RABINDRANATH TAGORE

SELECTED STORIES

SCHOLASTIC
New York Toronto London Auckland
Sydney New Delhi Hong Kong

Published by Scholastic India Pvt Ltd
A-27, Ground Floor, Sigma Centre
Infocity-1, Sector 34, Gurgaon 122001 (India)

This is a work of fiction. Names, characters, places and incidents are either the product of the author's imagination or are used fictitiously, and any resemblance to any actual persons, living or dead, events or locales is entirely coincidental.

Scholastic India is a subsidiary of Scholastic Inc., New York, 10012 (USA).
Publishers since 1920, with international operations in Canada, Australia, New Zealand, the United Kingdom, India and Hong Kong.

This edition: March 2018

ISBN-13: 978-93-5275-314-7

This reprint edition January 2026

Printed in India at Shivam Offset Press, New delhi

Contents

THE KABULIWALLAH

My five-year-old daughter Mini cannot live without chattering. I really believe that in all her life she has not wasted a minute in silence. Her mother is often angry because of this, and would stop her prattle, but I would not. To see Mini quiet is unnatural, and I cannot bear it long. And so my own talk with her is always lively.

One morning, for instance, when I was in the midst of the seventeenth chapter of my new novel, my little Mini stole into the room, and putting her hand into mine, said, 'Father! Ramdayal the doorkeeper calls a crow a krow! He doesn't know anything, does he?'

Before I could explain to her the differences of language in this world, she had already broached another subject. 'What do you think, Father? Bhola says there is an elephant in the clouds, blowing water out of his trunk, and that is why it rains!'

And then, darting off anew, while I sat still thinking

of some reply to this last, saying, 'Father! How is Mother related to you?'

'My dear little sister in the law!' I murmured involuntarily to myself, but with a grave face contrived to answer, 'Go and play with Bhola, Mini! I am busy!'

The window of my room overlooks the road. The child had seated herself at my feet near my table, and was playing softly, drumming on her knees. I was hard at work on my seventeenth chapter, where Protrap Singh, the hero, had just caught Kanchanlata, the heroine, in his arms, and was about to escape with her by the third storey window of the castle, when all of a sudden Mini left her play, and ran to the window, crying, 'A Kabuliwallah! A Kabuliwallah!' Sure enough, in the street below was a Kabuliwallah, passing slowly along. He wore the loose soiled clothing of his people, with a big turban; there was a bag on his back, and he carried boxes of grapes in his hand.

I cannot tell what my daughter's feelings at the sight of this man were, but she began to call him loudly. 'Ah!' I thought, 'he will come in, and my seventeenth chapter will never be finished!' At that exact moment the Kabuliwallah turned and looked up at the child. When she saw this, overcome by terror, she fled to her mother's protection, and disappeared. She had a blind belief that inside the bag, which the big man carried, there were perhaps two or three other children like herself. The pedlar meanwhile entered my doorway, and greeted me with a smiling face.

So precarious was the position of my hero and my heroine, that my first impulse was to stop and buy something, since the man had been called. I made some small purchases, and a conversation began about Abdur Rahman, the Russians, the English and the Frontier Policy.

As he was about to leave, he asked, 'And where is the little girl, sir?'

And I, thinking that Mini must get rid of her false fear, had her brought out.

She stood by my chair and looked at the Kabuliwallah and his bag. He offered her nuts and raisins, but she would not be tempted, and only clung closer to me, with all her doubts increased.

This was their first meeting.

One morning, however, not many days later, as I was leaving the house, I was startled to find Mini seated on a bench near the door, laughing and talking, with the great Kabuliwallah at her feet. In all her life, it appeared, my small daughter had never found so patient a listener, save her father. And already the corner of her little sari was stuffed with almonds and raisins, the gift of her visitor. 'Why did you give her those?' I asked, and taking out an eight-anna bit, I handed it to him. The man accepted the money without demur, and slipped it into his pocket.

Alas, on my return an hour later, I found the unfortunate

coin had made twice its own worth of trouble! For the Kabuliwallah had given it to Mini, and her mother catching sight of the bright round object, had pounced on the child with 'Where did you get that eight-anna bit?'

'The Kabuliwallah gave it to me,' said Mini cheerfully.

'The Kabuliwallah gave it to you!' cried her mother, shocked. 'Oh Mini! How could you take it from him?'

I, entering at the moment, saved her from impending disaster, and proceeded to make my own inquiries.

It was not the first or second time, I found, that the two had met. The Kabuliwallah had overcome the child's first terror by a judicious bribery of nuts and almonds, and the two were now great friends.

They had many quaint jokes which afforded them much amusement. Seated in front of him, looking down on his gigantic frame in all her tiny dignity, Mini would ripple her face with laughter, and begin, 'O Kabuliwallah, Kabuliwallah, what have you got in your bag?'

And he would reply in the nasal accents of the mountaineer, 'An elephant!' Not much cause for merriment, perhaps; but how they both enjoyed the witticism! And for me, this child's talk with a grown-up man had always in it something strangely fascinating.

Then the Kabuliwallah, not to be behind, would take his turn, 'Well, little one, and when are you going to the father-in-law's house?'

Now most small Bengali maidens have heard long ago

about the father-in-law's house; but we, being a little new-fangled, had kept these things from our child, and Mini at this question must have been a trifle bewildered. But she would not show it, and with ready tact replied, 'Are you going there?'

Amongst men of the Kabuliwallah's class, however, it is well known that the words father-in-law's house have a double meaning. It is an euphemism for jail, the place where we are well cared for, at no expense to ourselves. In this sense would the sturdy pedlar take my daughter's question. 'Ah,' he would say, shaking his fist at an invisible policeman, 'I will thrash my father-in-law!' Hearing this, and picturing the poor discomfited relative, Mini would go off into peals of laughter, in which her formidable friend would join.

These were autumn mornings, the very time of year when kings of old went forth to conquest; and I, never stirring from my little corner in Calcutta, would let my mind wander over the whole world. At the very name of another country, my heart would go out to it, and at the sight of a foreigner in the streets, I would fall to weaving a network of dreams—the mountains, the glens and the forests of his distant home, with his cottage in its setting, and the free and independent life of far-away wilds. Perhaps the scenes of travel conjure themselves up before me, and pass and repass in my imagination all the more vividly, because I lead such a vegetable existence that a call to travel would fall upon me like a thunderbolt. In the presence of this Kabuliwallah, I was immediately transported to the foot of arid mountain peaks, with narrow little defiles twisting in and out amongst their towering heights. I could see the string of camels bearing the merchandise, and the company of turbaned merchants, carrying some of their queer old firearms, and some of their spears, journeying downward towards the plains. I could see—but at some such point Mini's mother would intervene, imploring me to "beware of that man".

Mini's mother is unfortunately a very timid lady. Whenever she hears a noise in the street, or sees people coming towards the house, she always jumps to the conclusion that they are either thieves or drunkards or snakes or tigers or malaria or cockroaches or caterpillars or an English sailor. Even after all these years of experience, she is not able to overcome her terror. So she was full of doubts about the Kabuliwallah, and used to beg me to keep a watchful eye on him.

I tried to laugh her fear gently away, but then she would turn round on me seriously, and ask me solemn questions.

Were children never kidnapped?

Was it, then, not true that there was slavery in Kabul?

Was it so very absurd that this big man should be able to carry off a tiny child?

I urged that, though not impossible, it was highly

improbable. But this was not enough, and her dread persisted. As it was indefinite, however, it did not seem right to forbid the man to come to the house, and the intimacy grew unchecked.

Once a year in the middle of January, Rahmun, the Kabuliwallah, was in the habit of returning to his country, and as the time approached, he would be very busy, going from house to house collecting his debts. This year, however, he could always find time to come and see Mini. It would have seemed to an outsider that there was some conspiracy between the two, for when he could not come in the morning, he would appear in the evening.

Even to me it was a little startling now and then, in the corner of a dark room, suddenly to see this tall, loose-garmented, man; but when Mini would run in smiling, with her, 'O! Kabuliwallah! Kabuliwallah!' and the two friends, so far apart in age, would subside into their old laughter and their old jokes, I felt reassured.

One morning, a few days before he had made up his mind to go, I was correcting my proof sheets in my study. It was chilly weather. Through the window the rays of the sun touched my feet, and the slight warmth was very welcome. It was almost eight o'clock, and the early pedestrians were returning home, with their heads covered. All at once, I heard an uproar in the street, and, looking out, saw Rahmun being led away bound between two policemen, and behind them a crowd of curious boys. There were blood stains on the clothes of the Kabuliwallah, and one of the policemen carried a knife. Hurrying out, I stopped them and enquired what it all meant. Partly from one, partly from another, I gathered that a certain neighbour had owed the pedlar something for a Rampuri shawl, but had falsely denied having bought it, and that in the course of the quarrel, Rahmun had struck him. Now in the heat of his excitement, the prisoner began calling his enemy all sorts of names, when suddenly in a verandah of my house appeared my little Mini, with her usual exclamation, 'O Kabuliwallah! Kabuliwallah!' Rahmun's face lighted up as he turned to her. He had no bag under his arm today, so she could not discuss the elephant with him. She at once therefore proceeded to the next question, 'Are you going to the father-in-law's house?' Rahmun laughed and said, 'Just where I am going, little one!' Then, seeing that the reply did not amuse the child, he held up his fettered hands. 'Ali,' he said, 'I would have thrashed that old father-in-law, but my hands are bound!'

On a charge of murderous assault, Rahmun was sentenced to some years' imprisonment.

Time passed away, and he was not remembered. The accustomed work in the accustomed place was ours, and the thought of the once-free mountaineer spending his years in prison seldom or never occurred to us. Even my light-hearted Mini, I am ashamed to say, forgot her old friend.

New companions filled her life. As she grew older, she spent more of her time with girls. So much time indeed did she spend with them that she came no more, as she used to do, to her father's room. I was scarcely on speaking terms with her.

Years had passed away. It was once more autumn and we had made arrangements for our Mini's marriage. It was to take place during the puja holidays. With Durga returning to Kailas, the light of our home also was to depart to her husband's house, and leave her father's in the shadow.

The morning was bright. After the rains, there was a sense of ablution in the air, and the sun rays looked like pure gold. So bright were they that they gave a beautiful radiance even to the sordid brick walls of our Calcutta lanes. Since early dawn today the wedding pipes had been sounding, and at each beat my own heart throbbed. The wail of the tune, Bhairavi, seemed to intensify my pain at the approaching separation. My Mini was to be married tonight.

From early morning, noise and bustle had pervaded the house. In the courtyard the canopy had to be slung on its bamboo poles; the chandeliers with their tinkling sound must be hung in each room and verandah. There was no end of hurry and excitement. I was sitting in my study, looking through the accounts, when someone entered, saluting respectfully, and stood before me. It was Rahmun the Kabuliwallah. At first I did not recognise him. He had no bag, nor the long hair, nor the same vigour that he used to have. But he smiled, and I knew him again.

'When did you come, Rahmun?' I asked him.

'Last evening,' he said, 'I was released from jail.'

The words struck harsh upon my ears. I had never before talked with one who had wounded his fellow, and my heart shrank within itself, when I realised this, for I felt that the day would have been better-omened had he not turned up.

'There are ceremonies going on,' I said, 'and I am busy. Could you perhaps come another day?'

At once he turned to go; but as he reached the door he hesitated, and said, 'May I not see the little one, sir, for a moment?' It was his belief that Mini was still the same. He had pictured her running to him as she used, calling 'O Kabuliwallah! Kabuliwallah!' He had imagined too that they would laugh and talk together, just as of old. In fact, in memory of former days he had brought, carefully wrapped up in paper, a few almonds and raisins and grapes, obtained somehow from a countryman, for his own little fund was dispersed.

I said again, 'There is a ceremony in the house, and you will not be able to see any one today.'

The man's face fell. He looked wistfully at me for a moment, said 'Good morning,' and went out. I felt a little sorry, and would have called him back, but I found he was returning of his own accord. He came close up to me holding out his offerings and said, 'I brought these few things, sir, for the little one. Will you give them to her?'

I took them and was going to pay him, but he caught my hand and said, 'You are very kind, sir! Keep me in your recollection. Do not offer me money! You have a little girl, I too have one like her in my own home. I think of her and bring fruits to your child, not to make a profit for myself.'

Saying this, he put his hand inside his big loose robe, and brought out a small and dirty piece of paper. With great care he unfolded this, and smoothed it out with both hands on my table. It bore the impression of a little hand. Not a photograph. Not a drawing. The impression of an ink-smeared hand laid flat on the paper. This touch of his own little daughter had been always on his heart, as he had come year after year to Calcutta, to sell his wares in the streets.

Tears came to my eyes. I forgot that he was a poor Kabuli fruit-seller, while I was—but no, what was I more than he? He also was a father. That impression of the hand of his little Parbati in her distant mountain home reminded me of my own little Mini.

I sent for Mini immediately from the inner apartment. Many difficulties were raised, but I would not listen. Clad in the red silk of her wedding day, with the sandal paste on her forehead, and adorned as a young bride, Mini came, and stood bashfully before me.

The Kabuliwallah looked a little staggered at the apparition. He could not revive their old friendship. At last he smiled and said, 'Little one, are you going to your father-in-law's house?'

But Mini now understood the meaning of the word 'father-in-law,' and she could not reply to him as of old. She flushed up at the question, and stood before him with her bride-like face turned down.

I remembered the day when the Kabuliwallah and my Mini had first met, and I felt sad. When she had gone, Rahmun heaved a deep sigh, and sat down on the floor. The idea had suddenly come to him that his daughter too must have grown in this long time, and that he would have to make friends with her anew. Assuredly he would not find her as he used to know her. And besides, what might not have happened to her in these eight years?

The marriage-pipes sounded, and the mild autumn sun streamed round us. But Rahmun sat in the little Calcutta lane, and saw before him the barren mountains of Afghanistan.

I took out a bank note, and gave it to him, saying, 'Go back to your own daughter, Rahmun, in your own country, and may the happiness of your meeting bring good fortune to my child!'

Having made this present, I had to curtail some of the

festivities. I could not have the electric lights I had intended, nor the military band, and the ladies of the house were despondent at it. But to me the wedding feast was all the brighter for the thought that in a distant land a long-lost father met again with his only child.

THE POSTMASTER

The postmaster first took up his duties in the village of Ulapur. Though the village was a small one, there was an indigo factory nearby, and the proprietor, an Englishman, had managed to get a post office established.

Our postmaster belonged to Calcutta. He felt like a fish out of water in this remote village. His office and living room were in a dark thatched shed, not far from a green, slimy pond, surrounded on all sides by a dense growth.

The men employed in the indigo factory had no leisure; moreover, they were hardly desirable companions for decent folk. Nor is a Calcutta boy an adept in the art of associating with others. Among strangers he appears either proud or ill at ease. At any rate, the postmaster had but little company; nor did he have much to do.

At times he tried his hand at writing a verse or two. That the movement of the leaves and the clouds of the sky were enough to fill life with joy—such were the sentiments to which he sought to give expression. But God knows that the poor fellow would have felt it as the gift of a new life, if some genie of the Arabian Nights had in one night swept away the trees, leaves and all, and replaced them with a macadamised road, hiding the clouds from view with rows of tall houses.

The postmaster's salary was small. He had to cook his own meals, which he used to share with Ratan, an orphan girl of the village, who did odd jobs for him.

When in the evening the smoke began to curl up from the village cow sheds, and the cicalas chirped in every bush; when the fakirs of the Baul sect sang their shrill songs in their daily meeting place, when any poet, who had attempted to watch the movement of the leaves in the dense bamboo thickets, would have felt a ghostly shiver run down his back, the postmaster would light his little lamp, and call out "Ratan".

Ratan would sit outside waiting for this call, and, instead of coming in at once, would reply, 'Did you call me, sir?'

'What are you doing?' the postmaster would ask.

'I must be going to light the kitchen fire,' would be the answer.

And the postmaster would say 'Oh, let the kitchen fire be for a while; light me my pipe first.'

At last Ratan would enter, with puffed-out cheeks, vigorously blowing into a flame a live coal to light the tobacco. This would give the postmaster an opportunity of conversing with her. 'Well, Ratan,' perhaps he would begin, 'do you remember anything of your mother?' That was a fertile subject. Ratan partly remembered, and partly didn't. Her father had been fonder of her than her mother; him she recollected more vividly. He used to come home in the evening after his work, and one or two evenings stood out more clearly than others, like pictures in her memory. Ratan would squat on the floor near the postmaster's feet, as memories crowded in upon her. She called to mind a little brother that she had—and how on some bygone cloudy day she had played at fishing with him on the edge of the pond, with a twig for a make-believe fishing rod. Such little incidents would drive out greater events from her mind. Thus, as they talked, it would often get very late, and the postmaster would feel too lazy to do any cooking at all. Ratan would then hastily light the fire, and toast some unleavened bread, which, with the cold remnants of the morning meal, was enough for their supper.

On some evenings, seated at his desk in the corner of the big empty shed, the postmaster too would call up memories of his own home, of his mother and his sister, of those for whom in his exile his heart was sad—memories which were always haunting him, but which he could not talk about with the men of the factory, though he found himself naturally recalling them aloud in the presence of the simple little girl.

And so it came about that the girl would allude to his people as mother, brother and sister, as if she had known them all her life. In fact, she had a complete picture of each one of them painted in her little heart.

One noon, during a break in the rains, there was a cool soft breeze blowing; the smell of the damp grass and leaves in the hot sun felt like the warm breathing of the tired earth on one's body. A persistent bird went on all the afternoon repeating the burden of its one complaint in Nature's audience chamber.

The postmaster had nothing to do. The shimmer of the freshly washed leaves, and the banked-up remnants of the retreating rain clouds were sights to see; and the postmaster was watching them, and thinking to himself, 'Oh, if only some kindred soul were near—just one loving human being whom I could hold near my heart!' This was exactly, he went on to think, what that bird was trying to say, and it was the same feeling which the murmuring leaves were striving to express. But no one knows, or would believe, that such an idea might also take possession of an ill-paid village postmaster in the deep, silent mid-day interval of his work.

The postmaster sighed, and called Ratan. Ratan was then sprawling beneath the guava tree, busily engaged in eating unripe guavas. At the voice of her master, she ran up breathlessly, saying, 'Were you calling me, Dada?'

‘I was thinking,’ said the postmaster, ‘of teaching you to read.’ And then for the rest of the afternoon he taught her the alphabet.

Thus, in a very short time, Ratan had got as far as the double consonants.

It seemed as though the showers of the season would never end. Canals, ditches and hollows were all overflowing with water. Day and night the patter of rain was heard, and the croaking of frogs. The village roads became impassable, and marketing had to be done in punts.

One heavily clouded morning, the postmaster’s little pupil had been long waiting outside the door for her call, but, not hearing it as usual, she took up her dog-eared book, and slowly entered the room. She found her master stretched out on his pallet, and, thinking he was resting, she was about to retire on tip-toe, when she suddenly heard her name—‘Ratan!’ She turned at once and asked, ‘Were you sleeping, Dada?’

The postmaster in a plaintive voice said, ‘I am not well. Feel my head; is it very hot?’

In the loneliness of his exile, and in the gloom of the rains, his ailing body needed a little tender nursing. He longed to remember the touch on the forehead of soft hands with tinkling bracelets, to imagine the presence of loving womanhood, the nearness of mother and sister. And the exile was not disappointed. Ratan ceased to be a little girl. She at once stepped into the post of mother, called in the village doctor, gave the patient his pills at the proper intervals, sat up all night by his pillow, cooked his meal for him, and every now and then asked, 'Are you feeling a little better, Dada?'

It was some time before the postmaster, with weakened body, was able to leave his sick bed. 'No more of this,' said he with decision. 'I must get a transfer.' He at once wrote off to Calcutta an application for a transfer, on the ground of the unhealthiness of the place.

Relieved from her duties as nurse, Ratan again took up her old place outside the door. But she no longer heard the same old call. She would sometimes peep inside furtively to find the postmaster sitting on his chair, or stretched on his pallet, and staring absent-mindedly into the air. While Ratan was awaiting her call, the postmaster was awaiting a reply to his application. The girl read her old lessons over and over again—her great fear was lest, when the call came, she might be found wanting in the double consonants. At last, after a week, the call did come one evening. With an overflowing heart Ratan rushed into the room—'Were you calling me, Dada?'

The postmaster said, 'I am going away tomorrow, Ratan.'

'Where are you going, Dada?'

'I am going home.'

'When will you come back?'

'I am not coming back.'

Ratan asked no other question. The postmaster, of his own accord, went on to tell her that his application for a transfer had been rejected, so he had resigned his post, and was going home.

For a long time neither of them spoke another word. The lamp went on dimly burning, and from a leak in one corner of the thatch water dripped steadily into an earthen vessel on the floor beneath it.

After a while Ratan rose, and went off to the kitchen to prepare the meal; but she was not so quick about it as on other days. Many new things to think of had entered her little brain. When the postmaster had finished his supper, the girl suddenly asked him, 'Dada, will you take me to your home?'

The postmaster laughed. 'What an idea!' said he; but he did not think it necessary to explain to the girl wherein lay the absurdity.

That whole night, in her waking and in her dreams, the postmaster's laughing reply haunted her—'What an idea!'

On getting up in the morning, the postmaster found his bath ready. He had stuck to his Calcutta habit of bathing in water drawn and kept in pitchers, instead of taking a plunge in the river as was the custom of the village. For some reason or the other, the girl could not ask him about the time of his departure, so she had fetched the water from the river long before sunrise, that it should be ready as early as he might want it. After the bath came a call for Ratan. She entered noiselessly, and looked silently into her master's face for orders. The master said, 'You need not be anxious about my going away, Ratan; I shall tell my successor to look after you.' These words were kindly meant, no doubt: but inscrutable are the ways of a woman's heart!

Ratan had borne many a scolding from her master without complaint, but these kind words she could not bear. She burst out weeping, and said, 'No, no, you need not tell anybody anything at all about me; I don't want to stay on here.'

The postmaster was dumbfounded. He had never seen Ratan like this before.

The new incumbent duly arrived, and the postmaster, having given over charge, prepared to depart. Just before starting he called Ratan, and said, 'Here is something for you; I hope it will keep you for some little time.' He brought out from his pocket the whole of his month's salary, retaining only a trifle for his travelling expenses. Then Ratan fell at his feet and cried, 'Oh, Dada, I pray you, don't give me anything, don't in any way trouble about me,' and then she ran away out of sight.

The postmaster heaved a sigh, took up his carpet bag, put his umbrella over his shoulder, and, accompanied by a man carrying his many-coloured tin trunk, he slowly made for the boat.

When he got in and the boat was under way, and the rain-swollen river, like a stream of tears welling up from the earth, swirled and sobbed at her bows, then he felt a sort of pain at heart; the grief-stricken face of a village girl seemed to represent for him the great unspoken pervading grief of Mother Earth herself. At one time he had an impulse to go back, and bring away along with him that lonesome waif, forsaken of the world. But the wind had just filled the sails, the boat had got well into the middle of the turbulent current, and already the village was left behind, and its outlying burning-ground came in sight.

So the traveller, borne on the breast of the swift-flowing river, consoled himself with philosophical reflections on the numberless meetings and partings going on in the world—on death, the great parting, from which none returns.

But Ratan had no philosophy. She was wandering about the post office in a flood of tears. It may be that she had still a lurking hope in some corner of her heart that her Dada would return, and that is why she could not tear herself away. Alas for the foolish human heart!

THE HOMECOMING

Phatik Chakravorti was the ringleader among the boys of the village. A new mischief got into his head. There was a heavy log lying on the mud-flat of the river waiting to be shaped into a mast for a boat. He decided that they should all work together to shift the log by force from its place and roll it away. The owner of the log would be angry and surprised, and they would all enjoy the fun. Every one seconded the proposal, and it was carried out unanimously.

But just as the fun was about to begin, Makhan, Phatik's younger brother, sauntered up and sat down on the log in front of them all without a word. The boys were puzzled for a moment. He was pushed, rather timidly, by one of the boys and told to get up but he remained quite unconcerned. He appeared like a young philosopher meditating on the futility of games. Phatik was furious. 'Makhan,' he cried, 'if you don't get down this minute, I'll thrash you!'

Makhan only moved to a more comfortable position.

Now, if Phatik was to keep his regal dignity before the public, it was clear he ought to carry out his threat. But his courage failed him at the crisis. His fertile brain, however, rapidly seized upon a new manoeuvre which would discomfit his brother and afford his followers an added amusement. He gave the word of command to roll the log and Makhan over together. Makhan heard the order, and made it a point of honour to stick on. But he overlooked the fact, like those who attempt earthly fame in other matters, that there was peril in it.

The boys began to heave at the log with all their might, calling out, 'One, two, three, go.' At the word "go" the log went; and with it went Makhan's philosophy, glory and all.

All the other boys shouted themselves hoarse with delight. But Phatik was a little frightened. He knew what was coming. And, sure enough, Makhan rose from Mother Earth blind as Fate and screaming like the Furies. He rushed at Phatik and scratched his face and beat him and kicked him, and then went crying home. The first act of the drama was over.

Phatik wiped his face, and sat down on the edge of a sunken barge on the river bank, and began to chew a piece of grass. A boat came up to the landing, and a middle-aged man, with grey hair and a dark moustache, stepped on shore. He saw the boy sitting there doing nothing, and asked him where the Chakravortis lived. Phatik went on chewing the grass, and said, 'Over there,' but it was quite impossible to tell where he pointed. The stranger asked him again. He swung his legs to and fro on the side of the barge, and said, 'Go and find out,' and continued to chew the grass as before.

But now a servant came down from the house and told Phatik his mother wanted him. Phatik refused to move. But the servant was the master on this occasion. He took Phatik up roughly, and carried him, kicking and struggling in impotent rage.

When Phatik came into the house, his mother saw him. She called out angrily, 'So you have been hitting Makhan again?'

Phatik answered indignantly, 'No, I haven't; who told you that?'

His mother shouted, 'Don't tell lies! You have.'

Phatik said suddenly, 'I tell you, I haven't. You ask Makhan!' But Makhan thought it best to stick to his previous statement. He said, 'Yes, mother. Phatik did hit me.'

Phatik's patience was already exhausted. He could not hear this injustice. He rushed at Makhan and hammered him with blows. 'Take that,' he cried, 'and that, and that, for telling lies.'

His mother took Makhan's side in a moment, and pulled Phatik away, beating him with her hands. When Phatik pushed her aside, she shouted out, 'You little villain! Would you hit your own mother?'

It was just at this critical juncture that the grey-haired stranger arrived. He asked what the matter was. Phatik looked sheepish and ashamed.

But when his mother stepped back and looked at the stranger, her anger was changed to surprise. For she recognised her brother, and cried, 'Why, Dada! Where have you come from?' As she said these words, she bowed to the ground and touched his feet. Her brother had gone away soon after she had married, and he had started some business in Bombay. Phatik's mother had lost her husband while he was in Bombay. Bishamber had now come back to Calcutta, and had at once made enquiries about his sister. He had then hastened to see her as soon as he had found out where she was.

The next few days were full of rejoicing. The brother asked after the education of the two boys. He was told by his sister that Phatik was a perpetual nuisance. He was lazy, disobedient and wild. But Makhan was as good as gold, as quiet as a lamb, and very fond of reading. Bishamber kindly offered to take Phatik off his sister's hands, and educate him with his own children in Calcutta. The widowed mother readily agreed. When his uncle asked Phatik if he would like to go to Calcutta with him, his joy knew no bounds, and he said, 'Oh, yes, uncle!' in a way that made it quite clear that he meant it.

It was an immense relief to the mother to get rid of Phatik. She had a prejudice against the boy, and no love was lost between the two brothers. She was in daily fear that he would either drown Makhan some day in the river or break his head in a fight or run him into some danger or the other. At the same time she was somewhat distressed to see Phatik's extreme eagerness to get away.

Phatik, as soon as all was settled, kept asking his uncle every minute when they were to start. He was on pins and needles all day long with excitement, and lay awake most of the night. He bequeathed to Makhan, in perpetuity, his fishing rod, his big kite and his marbles. Indeed, at his time of departure, his generosity towards Makhan was unbounded.

When they reached Calcutta, Phatik made the acquaintance of his aunt for the first time. She was by no means pleased with this unnecessary addition to her family. She found her own three boys quite enough to manage without taking anyone else. And to bring a village lad of fourteen into their midst was terribly upsetting. Bishamber should really have thought twice before committing such an indiscretion.

In this world of human affairs there is no worse nuisance than a boy at the age of fourteen. He is neither ornamental, nor useful. It is impossible to shower affection on him as on a little boy, and he is always getting in the way. If he talks with a childish lisp he is called a baby, and if he answers in a grown-up way he is called impertinent. In fact any talk at all from him is resented. Then he is at the unattractive, growing age. He grows out of his clothes with indecent haste, his voice grows hoarse and breaks and quavers, his face grows suddenly angular and unsightly. It is easy to excuse the shortcomings of early childhood, but it is hard to tolerate even unavoidable lapses in a boy of fourteen. The lad himself becomes painfully self-conscious. When he talks with elderly people he is either unduly forward, or else so unduly shy that he appears ashamed of his very existence.

Yet it is at this very age when in his heart of hearts a young lad most craves for recognition and love; and he becomes the devoted slave of anyone who shows him consideration. But none dare openly love him, for that would be regarded as undue indulgence, and therefore bad for the boy. So, what with scolding and chiding, he becomes very much like a stray dog that has lost his master.

For a boy of fourteen, his own home is the only paradise. To live in a strange house with strange people is little short of torture, while the height of bliss is to receive the kind looks of women, and never to be slighted by them.

It was anguish to Phatik to be the unwelcome guest in his aunt's house, despised by this elderly woman, and slighted on every occasion. If she ever asked him to do anything for her, he would be so overjoyed that he would overdo it; and then she would tell him not to be so stupid, but to get on with his lessons.

The cramped atmosphere of neglect in his aunt's house oppressed Phatik so much that he could hardly breathe. He wanted to go out into the open country and fill his lungs and breathe freely. But there was no open country to go to. Surrounded on all sides by Calcutta houses and walls, he would dream night after night of his village home, and long to be back there. He remembered the glorious meadow where he used to fly his kite all day long; the broad river banks where he would wander about the livelong day singing and shouting for joy; the narrow brook where he could go and dive and swim at any time he liked. He thought of his band of boy companions over whom he was despot. And, above all, the memory of that tyrant mother of his, who had such a prejudice against him, occupied him day and night. A kind of physical love like that of animals; a longing to be in the presence of the one who is loved, an inexpressible wistfulness during absence; a silent cry of the inmost heart for the mother, like the lowing of a calf in the twilight; this love, which was almost an animal instinct, agitated the shy, nervous, lean, uncouth and ugly boy. No one could understand it, but it preyed upon his mind continually.

There was no more backward boy in the whole school than Phatik. He gaped and remained silent when the teacher asked him a question, and like an overladen ass, patiently suffered all the blows that came down on his back. When other boys were out at play, he stood wistfully by the window and gazed at the roofs of the distant houses. And if by chance he espied children playing on the open terrace of any roof, his heart would ache with longing.

One day he summoned up all his courage and asked his uncle, 'Uncle, when can I go home?'

His uncle answered, 'Wait till the holidays come.' But the holidays would not come till November, and there was a long time still to wait.

One day Phatik lost his lesson book. Even with the help of books he had found it very difficult indeed to prepare his lesson. Now it was impossible. Day after day the teacher would cane him unmercifully. His condition became so abjectly miserable that even his cousins were ashamed to own him. They began to jeer and insult him more than the other boys. He went to his aunt at last, and told her that he had lost his book.

His aunt pursed her lips in contempt, and said, 'You great clumsy country lout! How can I afford, with all my family, to buy you new books five times a month?'

That night, on his way back from school, Phatik had a bad headache with a fit of shivering. He felt he was going to have an attack of malarial fever. His one great fear was that he would be a nuisance to his aunt.

The next morning Phatik was nowhere to be seen. All searches in the neighbourhood proved futile. The rain had been pouring in torrents all night, and those who went out in search of the boy got drenched through to the skin. At last Bishamber asked help from the police.

At the end of the day a police van stopped at the door before the house. It was still raining, and the streets were all flooded. Two constables brought out Phatik in their arms and placed him before Bishamber. He was wet through from head to foot, muddy all over, his face and eyes flushed red with fever, and his limbs all trembling. Bishamber carried him in his arms, and took him into the inner apartments. When his wife saw him, she exclaimed, 'What a heap of trouble this boy has given us. Hadn't you better send him home?'

Phatik heard her words and sobbed out loud, 'Uncle, I was just going home; but they dragged me back again.'

The fever rose very high, and all that night the boy was delirious. Bishamber brought in a doctor. Phatik opened his eyes flushed with fever, and looked up to the ceiling, and said vacantly, 'Uncle, have the holidays come yet? May I go home?'

Bishamber wiped the tears from his own eyes. He took Phatik's lean and burning hands in his own, and sat by him through the night. The boy began again to mutter. At last his voice became excited. 'Mother,' he cried, 'don't beat me like that! Mother! I am telling the truth!'

The next day Phatik gained consciousness for a short time. He turned his eyes about the room, as if expecting someone to come. At last, with an air of disappointment, his head sank back on the pillow. He turned his face to the wall with a deep sigh.

Bishamber knew his thoughts, and, bending down his head, whispered, 'Phatik, I have sent for your mother.' The day went by. The doctor said in a troubled voice that the boy's condition was very critical.

Phatik began to cry out, 'By the mark—three fathoms. By the mark—four fathoms. By the mark—' He had heard the sailor on the river-steamer calling out the mark on the plumb-line. Now he was himself plumbing an unfathomable sea.

Later in the day Phatik's mother burst into the room like a whirlwind, and began to toss from side to side and moan and cry in a loud voice.

Bishamber tried to calm her agitation, but she flung herself on the bed, and cried, 'Phatik, my darling, my darling.'

Phatik stopped his restless movements for a moment. His hands ceased beating up and down. He said, 'Eh?'

The mother cried again, 'Phatik, my darling, my darling.'

Phatik very slowly turned his head and, without seeing anybody, said, 'Mother, the holidays have come.'

MASTER MASHAI

I

Adhar Babu lived upon the interest of the capital left him by his father. Only the brokers, negotiating loans, came to his drawing room and smoked the silver-chased hookah, and the clerks from the attorney's office discussed the terms of some mortgage or the amount of the stamp fees. He was so careful with his money that even the most dogged efforts of the boys from the local football club failed to make any impression on his pocket.

At the time this story opens a new guest came into his household. After a long period of despair, his wife, Nanibala, bore him a son.

The child resembled his mother—large eyes, well-formed nose and fair complexion. Ratikanta, Adharlal's protégé, gave the verdict, 'He is worthy of this noble house.' They named him Venugopal.

Never before had Adharlal's wife expressed any opinion differing from her husband's on household expenses. There had been a hot discussion now and then about the propriety of some necessary item and up to this time she had merely acknowledged defeat with silent contempt. But now Adharlal could no longer maintain his supremacy. He had to give way little by little when things for his son were in question.

II

As Venugopal grew up, his father gradually became accustomed to spending money on him. He obtained an old teacher, who had a considerable repute for his learning and also for his success in dragging impassable boys through their examinations. But such a training does not lead to the cultivation of amiability. This man tried his best to win the boy's heart, but the little that was left in him of the natural milk of human kindness had turned sour, and the child repulsed his advances from the very beginning. The mother, in consequence, objected to him strongly, and complained that the very sight of him made her boy ill. So the teacher left.

Just then, Haralal made his appearance with a dirty dress and a torn pair of old canvas shoes. Haralal's mother, who was a widow, had kept him with great difficulty at a district school out of the scanty earnings which she made by cooking in people's houses and husking rice. He managed to pass the matriculation and determined to go to college. As a result of his half-starved condition, his pinched face tapered to a point in an unnatural manner—like Cape Comorin in the map of India; and the only broad portion of it was his forehead, which resembled the ranges of the Himalayas.

The servant asked Haralal what he wanted, and he answered timidly that he wished to see the master.

The servant answered sharply, 'You can't see him.' Haralal was hesitating, at a loss what to do next, when Venugopal, who had finished his game in the garden, suddenly came to the door. The servant shouted at Haralal, 'Get away.'

Quite unaccountably Venugopal grew excited and cried, 'No, he shan't get away.' And he dragged the stranger to his father.

Adharlal had just risen from his mid-day sleep and was sitting quietly on the upper verandah in his cane chair, rocking his legs. Ratikanta was enjoying his hookah, seated in a chair next to him. He asked Haralal how far he had got in his reading. The young man bent his head and answered that he had passed the matriculation. Ratikanta looked stern and expressed surprise that he should be so backward for his age. Haralal kept silence. It was Ratikanta's special pleasure to torture his patron's dependants, whether actual or potential.

Suddenly it struck Adharlal that he would be able to employ this youth as a tutor for his son on next to nothing.

He agreed, there and then, to take him at a salary of five rupees a month with boarding and lodging free.

III

This time the post of tutor remained occupied longer than before. From the very beginning of their acquaintance Haralal and his pupil became great friends. Never before did Haralal have such an opportunity of loving any young human creature. His mother had been so poor and dependent that he had never had the privilege of playing with the children where she had been employed at work. He had not hitherto suspected the hidden stores of love which lay accumulating all the while in his own heart.

Venu also was glad to find a companion in Haralal. He was the only boy in the house. His two younger sisters were looked down upon as unworthy of being his playmates. So his new tutor became his only companion, patiently bearing the undivided weight of the tyranny of his child friend.

IV

Venu was now eleven. Haralal had passed his intermediate, winning a scholarship. He was working hard for his BA degree. After college lectures were over, he would take Venu out into the public park and tell him stories about the heroes from Greek history and Victor Hugo's romances. The child used to get quite impatient to run to Haralal, after school hours, in spite of his mother's attempts to keep him by her side.

This displeased Nanibala. She thought that it was a deep-laid plot of Haralal's to captivate her boy, in order to prolong his own appointment. One day she talked to him from behind the purdah. 'It is your duty to teach my son only for an hour or two in the morning and evening. But why are you always with him? The child has nearly forgotten his own parents. You must understand that a man of your position is no fit companion for a boy belonging to this house.'

Haralal's voice choked a little as he answered that for the future he would merely be Venu's teacher and would keep away from him at other times.

It was Haralal's usual practice to begin his college study early before dawn. The child would come to him directly after he had washed himself. There was a small pool in the garden and they used to feed the fish in it with puffed rice. Venu was also engaged in building a miniature garden-house, at the corner of the garden, with its liliputian gates and hedges and gravel paths. When the sun became too hot they would go back into the house, and Venu would have his morning lesson from Haralal.

On the day in question Venu had risen earlier than usual, because he wished to hear the end of the story which Haralal had begun the evening before. But he found his teacher absent. When asked about him, the door servant said that he had gone out. At lesson time Venu remained unnaturally quiet. He never even asked Haralal why he had gone out, but went on mechanically with his lessons. When the child was with his mother taking his breakfast, she asked him what had happened to make him so gloomy, and why he was not eating his food. Venu gave no answer. After his meal his mother caressed him and questioned him repeatedly. Venu burst out crying and said, 'Master Mashai.' His mother asked Venu, 'What about Master Mashai?' But Venu found it difficult to name the offence which his teacher had committed.

His mother said to Venu, 'Has your Master Mashai been saying anything to you against me?'

Venu could not understand the question and went away.

V

There was a theft in Adhar Babu's house. The police were called in to investigate. Even Haralal's trunks were searched. Ratikanta said with meaning, 'The man who steals anything does not keep his thefts in his own box.'

Adharlal called his son's tutor and said to him, 'It will not be convenient for me to keep you in my own house. From today you will have to take up your quarters outside, only coming in to teach my son at the proper time.'

Ratikanta said sagely, drawing at his hookah, 'That is a good proposal—good for both parties.'

Haralal did not utter a word, but he sent a letter saying that it would no longer be possible for him to remain as tutor to Venu.

When Venu came back from school, he found his tutor's room empty. Even that broken steel trunk of his was absent. The rope was stretched across the corner, but there were no clothes or towel hanging on it. Only on the table, which formerly was strewn with books and papers, stood a bowl containing some goldfish with a label on which was written the word "Venu" in Haralal's handwriting. The boy ran up at once to his father and asked him what had happened. His father told him that Haralal had resigned his post. Venu went to his room and flung himself down and began to cry. Adharlal did not know what to do with him.

The next day, when Haralal was sitting on his wooden bedstead in the hostel, debating with himself whether he should attend his college lectures, suddenly he saw Adhar Babu's servant coming into his room followed by Venu. Venu at once ran up to him and threw his arms round his neck asking him to come back to the house.

Haralal could not explain why it was absolutely impossible for him to go back, but the memory of those clinging arms and that pathetic request used to choke his breath with emotion long after.

VI

Haralal found out, after this, that his mind was in an unsettled state, and that he had but a small chance of winning the scholarship, even if he could pass the examination. At the same time, he knew that, without the scholarship, he could not continue his studies. So he tried to get employment in some office.

Fortunately for him, an English manager of a big merchant firm took a fancy to him at first sight. After only a brief exchange of words the manager asked him if he had had any experience, and could he bring any testimonial. Haralal could only answer 'No'; nevertheless a post was offered him of twenty rupees a month and fifteen rupees were allowed him in advance to help him to come properly dressed to the office.

The manager made Haralal work extremely hard. He had to stay on after office hours and sometimes go to his master's house late in the evening. But, in this way, he learnt his work quicker than others, and his fellow clerks became jealous of him and tried to injure him, but without effect. He rented a small house in a narrow lane and brought his mother to live with him as soon as his salary was raised to forty rupees a month. Thus happiness came back to his mother after weary years of waiting.

Haralal's mother used to express a desire to see

Venugopal, of whom she had heard so much. She wished to prepare some dishes with her own hand and to ask him to come just once to dine with her son. Haralal avoided the subject by saying that his house was not big enough to invite him for that purpose.

VII

The news reached Haralal that Venu's mother had died. He could not wait a moment, but went at once to Adharlal's house to see Venu. After that they began to see each other frequently.

But times had changed. Venu, stroking his budding moustache, had grown into quite a young man of fashion. Friends, befitting his present condition, were numerous. That old dilapidated study chair and ink-stained desk had vanished, and the room now seemed to be bursting with pride at its new acquisitions—its looking-glasses, oleographs and other furniture. Venu had entered college, but showed no haste in crossing the boundary of the Intermediate examination.

Haralal remembered his mother's request to invite Venu to dinner. After great hesitation, he did so. Venugopal, with his handsome face, at once won the mother's heart. But as soon as ever the meal was over he became impatient to go, and looking at his gold watch he explained that he had pressing engagements elsewhere. Then he jumped into his carriage, which was waiting at the door, and drove away. Haralal with a sigh said to himself that he would never invite him again.

VIII

One day, on returning from office, Haralal noticed the presence of a man in the dark room on the ground floor of his house. Possibly he would have passed him by, had not the heavy scent of some foreign perfume attracted his attention. Haralal asked who it was, and the answer came,

'It is I, Master Mashai.'

'What is the matter, Venu?' said Haralal. 'When did you arrive?'

'I came hours ago,' said Venu. 'I did not know that you returned so late.'

They went upstairs together and Haralal lighted the lamp and asked Venu whether all was well. Venu replied that his college classes were becoming a fearful bore, and his father did not realise how dreadfully hard it was for him to go on in the same class, year after year, with students much younger than himself. Haralal asked him what he wished to do. Venu then told him that he wanted to go to England and become a barrister. He gave an instance of a student, much less advanced than himself, who was getting ready to go. Haralal asked him if he had received his father's permission. Venu replied that his father would not hear a word of it until he had passed the Intermediate, and that was an impossibility in his present frame of mind. Haralal suggested that he himself should go and try to talk to his father.

'No,' said Venu, 'I can never allow that!'

Haralal asked Venu to stay for dinner and while they were waiting, he gently placed his hand on Venu's shoulder and said, 'Venu, you should not quarrel with your father, or leave home.'

Venu jumped up angrily and said that if he was not welcome, he could go elsewhere. Haralal caught him by the hand and implored him not to go away without taking his food. But Venu broke away and was just leaving the room when Haralal's mother brought the food in on a tray. On seeing Venu about to leave, she pressed him to remain, and he did so with bad grace.

While he was eating, the sound of a carriage stopping at the door was heard. First a servant entered the room with creaking shoes and then Adhar Babu himself. Venu's face became pale. The mother left the room as soon as she saw strangers enter. Adhar Babu called out to Haralal in a voice thick with anger,

'Ratikanta gave me full warning, but I could not believe that you had such devilish cunning hidden in you. So, you think you're going to live upon Venu? This is sheer kidnapping, and I shall prosecute you in the Police Court.'

Venu silently followed his father and went out of the house.

IX

The firm to which Haralal belonged began to buy up large quantities of rice and dal from the country districts. To pay for this, Haralal had to take the cash every Saturday morning by the early train and disburse it. There were special centres where the brokers and middlemen would come with their receipts and accounts for settlement. Some discussion had taken place in the office about Haralal being entrusted with this work, without any security, but the manager undertook all the responsibility and said that a security was not needed. This special work used to go on from the middle of December to the middle of April. Haralal would get back from it very late at night.

One day, after his return, he was told by his mother that Venu had called and that she had persuaded him to take his dinner at their house. This happened more than once. The mother said that it was because Venu missed his own mother, and tears came into her eyes as she spoke about it.

One day Venu waited for Haralal to return and had a long talk with him.

'Master Mashai!' he said, 'father has become so cantankerous of late that I cannot live with him any longer. And, besides, I know that he is getting ready to marry again. Ratikanta is seeking a suitable match, and they are always conspiring about it. There used to be a time when my father would get anxious, if I were absent from home even for a few hours. Now, if I am away for more than a week, he takes no notice—indeed he is greatly relieved. If this marriage takes place, I feel that I cannot live in the house any longer. You must show me a way out of this. I want to become independent.'

Haralal felt deeply pained, but he did not know how to help his former pupil. Venu said that he was determined to go to England and become a barrister. Somehow or the other he must get the passage money out of his father: he could borrow it on a note of hand and his father would have to pay when the creditors filed a suit. With this borrowed money he would get away, and when he was in England his father was certain to remit his expenses.

'But who is there,' Haralal asked, 'who would advance you the money?'

'You!' said Venu.

'I!' exclaimed Haralal in amazement.

'Yes,' said Venu, 'I've seen the servant bringing heaps of money here in bags.'

'The servant and the money belong to someone else.'

Haralal explained why the money came to his house at night, like birds to their nest, to be scattered next morning.

'But can't the Manager advance the sum?' Venu asked.

'He may do so,' said Haralal, 'if your father stands security.'

The discussion ended at this point.

X

One Friday night a carriage and pair stopped before Haralal's lodging house. When Venu was announced, Haralal was counting money in his bedroom, seated on the floor. Venu entered the room dressed in a strange manner. He had discarded his Bengali dress and was wearing a Parsee coat and trousers and had a cap on his head. Rings were prominent on almost all the fingers of both hands, and a thick gold chain was hanging round his neck: there was a gold watch in his pocket, and diamond studs could be seen peeping from his shirt sleeves. Haralal at once asked him what the matter was and why he was wearing that dress.

'My father's marriage,' said Venu, 'will take place to-morrow. He tried hard to keep it from me, but I found it out. I asked him to allow me to go to our garden house at Barrackpur for a few days, and he was only too glad to get rid of me so easily. I am going there, and I wish to God I had never to come back.'

Haralal looked pointedly at the rings on his fingers. Venu explained that they had belonged to his mother. Haralal then asked him if he had already had his dinner. He answered, 'Yes, haven't you had yours?'

'No,' said Haralal, 'I cannot leave this room until I have all the money safely locked up in this iron chest.'

'Go and have dinner,' said Venu, 'while I keep guard here; your mother will be waiting for you.'

For a moment Haralal hesitated, and then he went out and had his dinner. In a short time he came back with his mother and the three of them sat among the bags of money talking together. When it was about midnight, Venu took out his watch and looked at it and jumped up saying that he would miss his train. Then he asked Haralal to keep all his rings and his watch and chain until he asked for them again. Haralal put them all together in a leather bag and laid it in the iron safe. Venu went out.

The canvas bags containing the currency notes had already been placed in the safe: only the loose coins remained to be counted over and put away with the rest.

XI

Haralal lay down on the floor of the same room, with the key under his pillow, and went to sleep. He dreamt that Venu's mother was loudly reproaching him from behind the curtain.

Her words were indistinct, but rays of different colours from the jewels on her body kept piercing the curtain like needles and violently vibrating. Haralal struggled to call Venu, but his voice seemed to forsake him. At last, with a noise, the curtain fell down. Haralal started up from his sleep and found darkness piled up round about him. A sudden gust of wind had flung open the window and put out the light. Haralal's whole body was wet with perspiration. He relighted the lamp and saw, by the clock, that it was four in the morning. There was no time to sleep again; for he had to get ready to start.

After Haralal had washed his face and hands his mother called from her own room, 'Baba, why are you up so soon?'

It was the habit of Haralal to see his mother's face the first thing in the morning in order to bring a blessing upon the day. His mother said to him, 'I was dreaming that you were going out to bring back a bride for yourself.' Haralal went to his own bedroom and began to take out the bags containing the silver and the currency notes.

Suddenly his heart stopped beating. Three of the bags appeared to be empty. He knocked them against the iron safe, but this only proved his fear to be true. He opened them and shook them with all his might. Two letters from Venu dropped out from one of the bags. One was addressed to his father and one to Haralal.

Haralal tore open his own letter and began reading. The words seemed to run into one another. He trimmed the lamp, but felt as if he could not understand what he read. Yet the purpose of the letter was clear. Venu had taken three thousand rupees, in currency notes, and had started for England. The steamer was to sail before daybreak that very morning. The letter ended with the words 'I am explaining everything in a letter to my father. He will pay off the debt; and then, again, my mother's ornaments, which I have left in your care, will more than cover the amount I have taken.'

Haralal locked up his room and hired a carriage and went with all haste to the jetty. But he did not know the name of the steamer which Venu had taken. He ran the whole length of the wharves from Prinsep Ghat to Metiaburuj. He found that two steamers had started on their voyage to England early that morning. It was impossible for him to know which of them carried Venu, or how to reach him.

When Haralal got home, the sun was strong and the whole of Calcutta was awake. Everything before his eyes seemed blurred. He felt as if he were pushing against a fearful obstacle which was bodiless and without pity. His mother came on the verandah to ask him anxiously where he had gone. With a dry laugh he said to her, 'To bring home a bride for myself,' and then he fainted.

On opening his eyes after a while, Haralal asked his mother to leave him alone. Entering his room he shut the door from inside while his mother remained seated on the floor of the verandah in the fierce glare of the sun. She kept calling to him fitfully, almost mechanically, 'Baba, Baba!'

The servant came from the manager's office and knocked at the door, saying that they would miss the train if they did not start out at once. Haralal called from inside, 'It will not be possible for me to start this morning.'

'Then when are we to go, sir?'

'I will tell you later on.'

The servant went downstairs with a gesture of impatience.

Suddenly Haralal thought of the ornaments which Venu had left behind. Up till now he had completely forgotten about them, but with the thought came instant relief. He took the leather bag containing them, and also Venu's letter to his father, and left the house.

Before he reached Adharlal's house he could hear the bands playing for the wedding, yet on entering he could feel that there had been some disturbance. Haralal was told that there had been a theft the night before and one or two servants were suspected. Adhar Babu was sitting in the upper verandah flushed with anger and Ratikanta was smoking his hookah. Haralal said to Adhar Babu, 'I have something private to tell you.'

Adharlal flared up, 'I have no time now!' He was afraid that Haralal had come to borrow money or to ask his help. Ratikanta suggested that if there was any delicacy in making the request in his presence he would leave the place. Adharlal told him angrily to sit where he was. Then Haralal handed over the bag which Venu had left behind. Adharlal asked what was inside it and Haralal opened it and gave the contents into his hands.

Then Adhar Babu said with a sneer, 'It's a paying business that you two have started—you and your former pupil! You were certain that the stolen property would be traced, and so you come along with it to me to claim a reward!'

Haralal presented the letter which Venu had written to his father. This only made Adharlal all the more furious.

'What's all this?' he shouted, 'I'll call for the police! My son has not yet come of age, and you have smuggled him out of the country! I'll bet my soul you've lent him a few hundred rupees, and then taken a note of hand for three thousand! But I am not going to be bound by this!'

'I never advanced him any money at all,' said Haralal.

'Then how did he find it?' said Adharlal, 'Do you mean to tell me he broke open your safe and stole it?'

Haralal stood silent.

Ratikanta sarcastically remarked, 'I don't believe this fellow ever set hands on as much as three thousand rupees in his life.'

When Haralal left the house he seemed to have lost the power of dreading anything, or even of being anxious. His mind seemed to refuse to work. Directly he entered the lane he saw a carriage waiting before his own lodging. For a moment he felt certain that it was Venu's. It was impossible to believe that his calamity could be so hopelessly final.

Haralal went up quickly, but found an English assistant from the firm sitting inside the carriage. The man came out when he saw Haralal and took him by the hand and asked him, 'Why didn't you go out by train this morning?' The servant had told the manager his suspicions and he had sent this man to find out.

Haralal answered, 'Notes to the amount of three thousand rupees are missing.'

The man asked how that could have happened.

Haralal remained silent.

The man said to Haralal, 'Let us go upstairs together and see where you keep your money.' They went up to the room and counted the money and made a thorough search of the house.

When the mother saw this she could not contain herself any longer. She came out before the stranger and said, 'Baba, what has happened?' He answered in broken Hindustani that some money had been stolen.

'Stolen!' the mother cried. 'Why! How could it be stolen? Who could do such a dastardly thing?'

Haralal said to her, 'Mother, don't say a word.'

The man collected the remainder of the money and told Haralal to come with him to the manager. The mother barred the way and said, 'Sir, where are you taking my son? I have brought him up, starving and straining to do honest work.

My son would never touch money belonging to others.'

The Englishman, not knowing Bengali, said, 'Achcha! Achcha!' Haralal told his mother not to be anxious; he would explain it all to the manager and soon be back again. The mother entreated him, with a distressed voice,

'Baba, you haven't taken a morsel of food all morning.' Haralal stepped into the carriage and drove away, and the mother sank to the ground in the anguish of her heart.

The manager said to Haralal, 'Tell me the truth. What happened?'

Haralal said to him, 'I haven't taken any money.'

'I believe you,' said the manager, 'but surely you know who has taken it.'

Haralal looked on the ground and remained silent.

'Somebody,' said the manager, 'must have taken it away with your connivance.'

'Nobody,' replied Haralal, 'could take it away with my knowledge without first taking my life.'

'Look here, Haralal,' said the manager, 'I trusted you completely. I took no security. I employed you in a post of great responsibility. Every one in the office was against it. The money is a small matter, but the shame of all this to me is a great matter. I will do one thing. I will give you the whole day to bring back this money. If you do so, I shall say nothing about it and I will keep you on in your post.'

It was now eleven o'clock. Haralal with bent head went

out of the office. The clerks began to discuss the affair with exultation.

'What can I do? What can I do?' Haralal repeated to himself as he walked along like one dazed, the sun's heat pouring down upon him. At last his mind ceased to think at all about what could be done, but the mechanical walk went on without ceasing.

This city of Calcutta, which offered its shelter to thousands and thousands of men, had become like a steel trap for him. He could see no way out. The whole body of people were conspiring to surround and hold him captive—this most insignificant of men, whom no one knew. Nobody had any special grudge against him, yet everybody was his enemy. The crowd passed by, brushing against him: the clerks of the offices were eating their lunch on the roadside from their plates made of leaves: a tired wayfarer on the Maidan, under the shade of a tree, was lying with one hand beneath his head and one leg raised over the other. The up-country women, crowded into hackney carriages, were wending their way to the temple: a chaprasi came up with a letter and asked him the address on the envelope—so the afternoon went by.

Then came the time when the offices were all about to close. Carriages started off in all directions, carrying people back to their homes. The clerks, packed tightly on the seats of the trams, looked at the theatre advertisements as they returned to their lodgings. From today, Haralal had neither his work in the office, nor release from work in the evening. He had no need to hurry to catch the tram to take him to his home. All the busy occupations of the city—the buildings, the horses and carriages, the incessant traffic, seemed, now at one time, to swell into dreadful reality, and at another time, to subside into the shadowy unreal.

Haralal had taken neither food, nor rest, nor shelter all that day.

The street lamps were lighted from one road to another and it seemed to him that a watchful darkness, like some demon, was keeping its eyes wide open to guard every movement of its victim. Haralal did not even have the energy to enquire how late it was. The veins on his forehead throbbed, and he felt as if his head would burst. Through the paroxysms of pain, which alternated with the apathy of dejection, only one thought came again and again to his mind; among the innumerable multitudes in that vast city, only one name found its way through his dry throat—"Mother!"

He said to himself, 'At the deep of night, when no one is awake to capture me—me, who am the least of all men, I will silently creep into my mother's arms and fall asleep, and may I never wake again!'

Haralal's one trouble was lest some police officer should molest him in the presence of his mother, and this kept him back from going home. When it became impossible for him at last to bear the weight of his own body, he hailed a carriage. The driver asked him where he wanted to go. He said, 'Nowhere. I want to drive across the Maidan to get some fresh air.' The man at first did not believe him and was about to drive on, when Haralal put a rupee into his hand as an advance payment. Thereupon the driver crossed, and then re-crossed the Maidan from one side to the other, traversing the different roads.

Haralal laid his throbbing head on the side of the open window of the carriage and closed his eyes. Slowly all the pain abated. His body became cool. A deep and intense peace filled his heart and a supreme deliverance seemed to embrace him on every side. It was not true—the day's despair which threatened him with its grip of utter helplessness. It was not true, it was false. He knew now that it was only an empty fear of the mind. Deliverance was in the infinite sky and there was no end to peace. No king or emperor in the world had the power to keep captive this non-entity, this Haralal. In the sky, surrounding his emancipated heart on every side, he felt the presence of his mother, that one poor woman. She seemed to grow and grow till she filled the infinity of darkness. All the roads and buildings and shops of Calcutta gradually became enveloped by her. In her presence vanished all the aching pains and thoughts and consciousness of Haralal. It burst—that bubble filled with the hot vapour of pain. And now there was neither darkness nor light, but only one tense fulness.

The Cathedral clock struck one. The driver called out impatiently, 'Babu, my horse can't go on any longer. Where do you want to go?'

There came no answer.

The driver came down and shook Haralal and asked him again where he wanted to go.

There came no answer.

And the answer was never received from Haralal, where he wanted to go.

ONCE THERE WAS A KING

When we were children there was no need to know who the king in the fairy story was. It didn't matter whether he was called Shiladitya or Shaliban, whether he lived at Kashi or Kanauj. The thing that made a seven-year-old boy's heart go thump, thump with delight was this one sovereign truth; this reality of all realities, 'Once there was a king.'

But the readers of this modern age are far more exact and exacting. When they hear such an opening to a story, they are at once critical and suspicious. They apply the searchlight of science to its legendary haze and ask, 'Which king?'

The storytellers have become more precise in their turn. They are no longer content with the old indefinite, 'There was a king,' but assume instead a look of profound learning, and begin, 'Once there was a king named Ajatasatru …'

The modern reader's curiosity, however, is not so easily

satisfied. He blinks at the author through his scientific spectacles, and asks again, 'Which Ajatasatru?'

'Every schoolboy knows,' the author proceeds, 'that there were three Ajatasatrus. The first was born in the twentieth century BC, and died at the tender age of two years and eight months. I deeply regret that it is impossible to find, from any trustworthy source, a detailed account of his reign. The second Ajatasatru is better known to historians. If you refer to the new Encyclopedia of History …'

By this time the modern reader's suspicions are dissolved. He feels he may safely trust his author. He says to himself, 'Now we shall have a story that is both improving and instructive.'

Ah! How we all love to be deluded! We have a secret dread of being thought ignorant. And we end by being ignorant after all, only we have done it in a long and roundabout way.

There is an English proverb, 'Ask me no questions, and I will tell you no lies.' The boy of seven who is listening to a fairy story understands that perfectly well; he withholds his questions while the story is being told. So the pure and beautiful falsehood of it all remains naked and innocent as a babe; transparent as truth itself; limpid as a fresh bubbling spring. But the ponderous and learned lie of our moderns has to keep its true character draped and veiled. And if there is discovered anywhere the least little peep-hole of deception, the reader turns away with a prudish disgust, and the author is discredited.

When we were young, we understood all sweet things; and we could detect the sweets of a fairy story by an unerring science of our own. We never cared for such useless things as knowledge. We only cared for truth. And our unsophisticated little hearts knew well where the Crystal Palace of Truth lay and how to reach it. But today we are expected to write pages of facts, while the truth is simply this,

'There was a king.'

I remember vividly that evening in Calcutta when the fairy story began. The rain and the storm had been incessant. The whole of the city was flooded. The water was knee-deep in our lane. I had a straining hope, which was almost a certainty, that my tutor would be prevented from coming that evening. I sat on the stool in the far corner of the veranda looking down the lane, with a heart beating faster and faster. Every minute I kept my eye on the rain, and when it began to grow less I prayed with all my might, 'Please, God, send some more rain till half past seven.' For I was quite ready to believe that there was no other need for rain except to protect one helpless boy one evening in one corner of Calcutta from the deadly clutches of his tutor.

If not in answer to my prayer, at any rate according to some grosser law of physical nature, the rain did not give up.

But, alas! Nor did my teacher.

Exactly to the minute, in the bend of the lane, I saw his approaching umbrella. The great bubble of hope burst in my breast, and my heart collapsed. Truly, if there is a punishment to fit the crime after death, then my tutor will be born again as me, and I shall be born as my tutor.

As soon as I saw his umbrella I ran as hard as I could to my mother's room. My mother and my grandmother were sitting opposite one another playing cards by the light of a lamp. I ran into the room, flung myself on the bed beside my mother, and said, 'Mother dear, the tutor has come, and I have such a bad headache; couldn't I have no lessons today?'

I hope no child of immature age will be allowed to read this story, and I sincerely trust it will not be used in text books or primers for schools. For what I did was dreadfully bad, and I received no punishment whatsoever. On the contrary, my wickedness was crowned with success.

My mother said to me, 'Alright,' and turning to the servant added, 'Tell the tutor that he can go back home.'

It was perfectly plain that she didn't think my illness very serious, as she went on with her game as before, and took no further notice. And I also, burying my head in the pillow, laughed to my heart's content. We perfectly understood one another, my mother and I.

But every one must know how hard it is for a boy of seven years to keep up the illusion of illness for a long time.

After about a minute I got hold of Grandmother and said, 'Grannie, do tell me a story.'

I had to ask this many times. Grannie and Mother went on playing cards, and took no notice. At last Mother said to me, 'Child, don't bother. Wait till we've finished our game.'

But I persisted. 'Grannie, do tell me a story.' I told Mother she could finish her game tomorrow, but she must let Grannie tell me a story then and there.

At last Mother threw down the cards and said, 'You had better do what he wants. I can't manage him.' Perhaps she had it in her mind that she would have no tiresome tutor on the morrow, while I should be obliged to be back to those stupid lessons.

As soon as Mother had given way, I rushed at Grannie. I got hold of her hand, and, dancing with delight, dragged her inside my mosquito curtain onto the bed. I clutched hold of the bolster with both hands in my excitement and jumped up and down with joy, and when I had got a little quieter, said, 'Now, Grannie, let's have the story!'

Grannie went on, 'And the king had a queen.' That was good to begin with. He had only one queen.

It is usual for kings in fairy stories to be extravagant in the number of queens. And whenever we hear that there are two queens, our hearts begin to sink. One is sure to be unhappy. But in Grannie's story that danger wasn't there. He had only one queen.

We next hear that the king had not got any son. At the age of seven I didn't think there was any need to bother if a man had had no son. He might only have been in the way. Nor are we greatly excited when we hear that the king has gone away into the forest to practise austerities in order to get a son. There was only one thing that would have made me go into the forest, and that was to get away from my tutor!

But the king left behind with his queen a small girl, who grew up into a beautiful princess.

Twelve years pass away, and the king goes on practising austerities, and never thinks all this while of his beautiful daughter. The princess has reached the full bloom of her youth. The age of marriage has passed, but the king does not return. And the queen pines away with grief and cries, 'Is my golden daughter destined to die unmarried? Ah me! What a fate is mine!'

Then the queen sent men to the king to entreat him earnestly to come back for a single night and take one meal in the palace. And the king consented.

The queen cooked with her own hand, with the greatest care, sixty four dishes, and made a seat for him of sandalwood, and arranged the food in plates of gold and cups of silver. The princess stood behind with the peacock-tail fan in her hand. The king, after twelve years' absence, came into the house, and the princess waved the fan, lighting up all the room with her beauty. The king looked in his daughter's face, and forgot to take his food.

At last he asked his queen, 'Pray, who is this girl whose beauty shines as the gold image of the goddess? Whose daughter is she?'

The queen beat her forehead and cried, 'Ah, how evil is my fate! Do you not know your own daughter?'

The king was struck with amazement. He said at last, 'My tiny daughter has grown to be a woman.'

'What else?' the queen said with a sigh. 'Do you not know that twelve years have passed by?'

'But why did you not give her in marriage?' asked the king.

'You were away,' the queen said. 'And how could I find her a suitable husband?'

The king became vehement with excitement. 'The first man I see tomorrow,' he said, 'when I come out of the palace, shall marry her.'

The princess went on waving her fan of peacock feathers, and the king finished his meal.

The next morning, as the king came out of his palace, he saw the son of a Brahmin gathering sticks in the forest outside the palace gates. His age was about seven or eight.

The king said, 'I will marry my daughter to him.'

Who can interfere with a king's command? At once the boy was called, and the marriage garlands were exchanged between him and the princess.

At this point I came up close to my wise Grannie and asked her eagerly, 'What then?'

In the bottom of my heart there was a devout wish to substitute myself for that fortunate wood-gatherer who was seven years old. The night was resonant with the patter of rain. The earthen lamp by my bedside was burning low. My grandmother's voice droned on as she told the story. And all these things served to create in a corner of my credulous heart the belief that I had been gathering sticks in the dawn of some indefinite time in the kingdom of some unknown king, and in a moment garlands had been exchanged between me and the princess, beautiful as the Goddess of Grace. She had a gold band on her hair and gold earrings in her ears. She had a necklace and bracelets of gold, and a golden waist-chain round her waist, and a pair of golden anklets tinkled above her feet.

If my grandmother were an author, how many explanations she would have to offer for this little story! First of all, every one would ask why the king remained twelve years in the forest. Secondly, why should the king's daughter remain unmarried all that while? This would be regarded as absurd.

Even if she could have got so far without a quarrel, still there would have been a great hue and cry about the marriage itself. First, it never happened. Secondly, how could there be a marriage between a princess of the Warrior Caste and a boy of the priestly Brahman Caste? Her readers would have imagined at once that the writer was preaching against our social customs in an underhand way. And they would write letters to the papers.

So I pray with all my heart that my grandmother may be born a grandmother again, and not through some cursed fate take birth as her luckless grandson.

So, with a throb of joy and delight, I asked Grannie, 'What then?'

Grannie went on, 'Then the princess took her little husband away in great distress, and built a large palace with seven wings, and began to cherish her husband with great care.'

I jumped up and down in my bed and clutched at the bolster more tightly than ever and said, 'What then?'

Grannie continued, 'The little boy went to school and learnt many lessons from his teachers, and as he grew up, his class-fellows began to ask him, "Who is that beautiful lady who lives with you in the palace with the seven wings?" The Brahman's son was eager to know who she was. He could only remember how one day he had been gathering sticks, and a great disturbance arose. But all that was so long ago that he had no clear recollection.

Four or five years passed in this way. His companions always asked him, "Who is that beautiful lady in the palace with the seven wings?"

And the Brahman's son would come back from school and sadly tell the princess, "My school companions always ask me who that beautiful lady in the palace with the seven wings is, and I can give them no reply. Tell me, oh, tell me who you are!"

The princess said, "Let it pass today. I will tell you some other day." And every day the Brahman's son would ask, "Who are you?" and the princess would reply, "Let it pass today. I will tell you some other day." In this manner four or five more years passed away.

At last the Brahman's son became very impatient and said, 'If you do not tell me today who you are, beautiful lady, I will leave this palace with the seven wings.'

Then the princess said, "I will certainly tell you tomorrow."

Next day the Brahman's son, as soon as he came home from school, said, 'Now tell me who you are.'

The princess said, "Tonight I will tell you after supper, when you are in bed."

The Brahman's son said "very well" and he began to count the hours in expectation of the night. And the princess, on her side, spread white flowers over the golden bed, and lighted a gold lamp with fragrant oil and adorned her hair, and dressed herself in a beautiful robe of blue, and began to count the hours in expectation of the night.

That evening when her husband, the Brahman's son, had finished his meal, too excited almost to eat, and had gone to the golden bed in the bedchamber strewn with flowers, he said to himself, "Tonight I shall surely know who this beautiful lady is in the palace with the seven wings."

The princess took for her the food that was left over by her husband, and slowly entered the bedchamber. She had to answer that night the question, who was the beautiful lady who lived in the palace with the seven wings. And as she went up to the bed to tell him, she found a serpent had crept out of the flowers and had bitten the Brahman's son. Her boy-husband was lying on the bed of flowers, with face pale in death.

My heart suddenly ceased to throb, and I asked with choking voice, 'What then?'

Grannie said, 'Then …'

But what is the use of going on any further with the story? It would only lead on to what was more and more impossible. The boy of seven did not know that. If there was some 'What then?' after death, no grandmother of a grandmother could tell us all about it.

But the child's faith never admits defeat, and it would snatch at the mantle of death itself to turn him back. It would be outrageous for him to think that such a story of one teacherless evening could so suddenly come to a stop. Therefore the grandmother had to call back her story from the ever-shut chamber of the great End, but she does it so simply: it is merely by floating the dead body on a banana stem on the river, and having some incantations read by a magician. But in that rainy night and in the dim light of a lamp, death loses all its horror in the mind of the boy, and seems nothing more than a deep slumber of a single night. When the story ends, the tired eyelids are weighed down with sleep. Thus it is that we send the little body of the child floating on the back of sleep over the still water of time, and then in the morning read a few verses of incantation to restore him to the world of life and light.

THE BABY

I

Raicharan was twelve years old when he came as a servant to his master's house. He belonged to the same caste as his master, and was given his master's little son to nurse. As time went on, the boy left Raicharan's arms to go to school. From school he went on to college, and after college he entered the judicial service. Always, until he married, Raicharan was his sole attendant.

But, when a mistress came into the house, Raicharan found two masters instead of one. All his former influence passed to the new mistress. This was compensated for by a fresh arrival. Anukul had a son born to him, and Raicharan, by his unsparing attentions, soon got a complete hold over the child. He used to toss him up in his arms, call to him in absurd baby language, put his face close to the baby's and draw it away again with a grin.

Presently the child was able to crawl and cross the

doorway. When Raicharan went to catch him, he would scream with mischievous laughter and make for safety. Raicharan was amazed at the profound skill and exact judgement the baby showed when pursued. He would say to his mistress with a look of awe and mystery, 'Your son will be a judge someday.'

New wonders came in their turn. When the baby began to toddle, that was to Raicharan an epoch in human history. When he called his father Ba-ba and his mother Ma-ma and Raicharan Chan-na, then Raicharan's ecstasy knew no bounds. He went out to tell the news to all the world.

After a while Raicharan was asked to show his ingenuity in other ways. He had, for instance, to play the part of a horse, holding the reins between his teeth and prancing with his feet. He had also to wrestle with his little charge, and if he could not, by a wrestler's trick, fall on his back defeated at the end, a great outcry was certain.

About this time Anukul was transferred to a district on the banks of the Padma. On his way through Calcutta he bought his son a little go-cart. He also bought him a yellow satin waistcoat, a gold-laced cap, and some gold bracelets and anklets. Raicharan was wont to take these out, and put them on his little charge with ceremonial pride, whenever they went for a walk.

Then came the rainy season, and day after day the rain poured down in torrents. The hungry river, like an enormous serpent, swallowed down terraces, villages, cornfields, and covered with its flood the tall grasses and wild casuarinas on the sand banks. From time to time there was a deep thud as the river banks crumbled. The unceasing roar of the rain current could be heard from far away. Masses of foam, carried swiftly past, proved to the eye the swiftness of the stream.

One afternoon the rain cleared. It was cloudy, but cool and bright. Raicharan's little despot did not want to stay in on such a fine afternoon. His lordship climbed into the go-cart. Raicharan, between the shafts, dragged him slowly along till he reached the rice fields on the banks of the river. There was no one in the fields, and no boat on the stream. Across the water, on the farther side, the clouds were rifted in the west. The silent ceremonial of the setting sun was revealed in all its glowing splendour. In the midst of that stillness, the child, all of a sudden, pointed with his finger in front of him and cried, 'Chan-nal Pitty fow.'

Close by on a mud flat stood a large Kadamba tree in full flower. My lord, the baby, looked at it with greedy eyes, and Raicharan knew his meaning. Only a short time before he had made, out of these very flower balls, a small go-cart; and the child had been so entirely happy dragging it about with a string, that for the whole day Raicharan was not made to put on the reins at all. He was promoted from a horse into a groom.

But Raicharan had no wish that evening to go splashing knee-deep through the mud to reach the flowers. So he quickly pointed his finger in the opposite direction, calling out, 'Oh, look, baby, look! Look at the bird.' And with all sorts of curious noises he pushed the go-cart rapidly away from the tree.

But a child, destined to be a judge, cannot be put off so easily. And besides, there was at the time nothing to attract his eyes. And you cannot keep up forever the pretence of an imaginary bird.

The little Master's mind was made up, and Raicharan was at his wits' end. 'Very well, baby,' he said at last, 'you sit still in the cart, and I'll go and get you the pretty flower. Only mind you don't go near the water.'

As he said this, he made his legs bare to the knee and waded through the oozing mud towards the tree.

The moment Raicharan had gone, his little Master went off at a racing speed to the forbidden water. The baby saw the river rushing by, splashing and gurgling as it went. It seemed as though the disobedient wavelets themselves were running away from some greater Raicharan with the laughter of a thousand children. At the sight of their mischief, the heart of the human child grew excited and restless. He got down stealthily from the go-cart and toddled off towards the river. On his way he picked up a small stick and leant over the bank of the stream pretending to fish. The mischievous fairies of the river with their mysterious voices seemed inviting him into their play house.

Raicharan had plucked a handful of flowers from the tree, and was carrying them back in the end of his cloth, with his face wreathed in smiles. But when he reached the go-cart, there was no one there. He looked on all sides and there was no one there. He looked back at the cart and there was no one there.

In that first terrible moment his blood froze within him. Before his eyes the whole universe swam round like a dark mist. From the depth of his broken heart he gave one piercing cry, 'Master, Master, little Master.'

But no voice answered 'Chan-na.' No child laughed mischievously back; no scream of baby delight welcomed his return. Only the river ran on, with its splashing, gurgling noise as before—as though it knew nothing at all, and had no time to attend to such a tiny human event as the death of a child.

As the evening passed by, Raicharan's mistress became very anxious. She sent men out on all sides to search. They went with lanterns in their hands, and reached at last the banks of the Padma. There they found Raicharan rushing up and down the fields, like a stormy wind, shouting the cry of despair, 'Master, Master, little Master!'

When they got Raicharan home at last, he fell prostrate at his mistress's feet. They shook him, and questioned him, and asked him repeatedly where he had left the child; but all he could say was that he knew nothing.

Though everyone held the opinion that the Padma had swallowed the child, there was a lurking doubt left in the mind. For a band of gypsies had been noticed outside the village that afternoon, and some suspicion rested on them. The mother went so far in her wild grief as to think it possible that Raicharan himself had stolen the child. She called him aside with piteous entreaty and said, 'Raicharan, give me back my baby. Oh! Give me back my child. Take from me any money you ask, but give me back my child!'

Raicharan only beat his forehead in reply. His mistress ordered him out of the house.

Anukul tried to reason his wife out of this wholly unjust suspicion. 'Why on earth,' he said, 'should he commit such a crime as that?'

The mother only replied, 'The baby had gold ornaments on his body. Who knows?'

It was impossible to reason with her after that.

II

Raicharan went back to his own village. Up to this time he had had no son, and there was no hope that any child would now be born to him. But it came about before the end of a year that his wife gave birth to a son and died.

All overwhelming resentment at first grew up in Raicharan's heart at the sight of this new baby. At the back of his mind was resentful suspicion that it had come as a usurper in place of the little Master. He also thought it would be a grave offence to be happy with a son of his own after what had happened to his master's little child. Indeed, if it had not been for a widowed sister, who mothered the new baby, it would not have lived long.

But a change gradually came over Raicharan's mind. A wonderful thing happened. This new baby in turn began to crawl about and cross the doorway with mischief in its face. It also showed an amusing cleverness in making its escape to safety. Its voice, its sounds of laughter and tears, its gestures, were those of the little Master. On some days, when Raicharan listened to its crying, his heart suddenly began thumping wildly against his ribs, and it seemed to him that his former little Master was crying somewhere in the unknown land of death because he had lost his Chan-na.

Phailna (for that was the name Raicharan's sister gave to the new baby) soon began to talk. It learnt to say Ba-ba and Ma-ma with a baby accent. When Raicharan heard those familiar sounds the mystery suddenly became clear. The little Master could not cast off the spell of his Chan-na, and therefore he had been reborn in his own house.

The arguments in favour of this were, to Raicharan, altogether beyond dispute:

Firstly, the new baby was born soon after his little master's death. Secondly, his wife could never have accumulated such merit as to give birth to a son in middle age. Lastly, the new baby walked with a toddle and called out Ba-ba and Ma-ma. There was no sign lacking which marked out the future judge.

Then suddenly Raicharan remembered that terrible accusation of the mother. 'Ah,' he said to himself with amazement, 'the mother's heart was right. She knew I had stolen her child.' When once he had come to this conclusion, he was filled with remorse for his past neglect. He now gave himself over, body and soul, to the new baby, and became its devoted attendant. He began to bring it up, as if it were the son of a rich man. He bought a go-cart, a yellow satin waistcoat, and a gold-embroidered cap. He melted down the ornaments of his dead wife and made gold bangles and anklets. He refused to let the little child play with anyone of the neighbourhood, and became himself its sole companion day and night. As the baby grew up to boyhood, he was so petted and spoilt and clad in such finery that the village children would call him Your Lordship and jeer at him; and older people regarded Raicharan as unaccountably crazy about the child.

At last the time came for the boy to go to school. Raicharan sold his small piece of land and went to Calcutta. There he got employment with great difficulty as a servant, and sent Phailna to school. He spared no pains to give him the best education, the best clothes, the best food. Meanwhile he lived himself on a mere handful of rice, and would say in secret, 'Ah! My little Master, my dear little Master, you loved me so much that you came back to my house. You shall never suffer from any neglect of mine.'

Twelve years passed away in this manner. The boy was able to read and write well. He was bright and healthy and good-looking. He paid a great deal of attention to his personal appearance, and was specially careful in parting his hair. He was inclined to extravagance and finery, and spent money freely. He could never quite look on Raicharan as a father, because, though fatherly in affection, he had the manner of a servant. A further fault was this that Raicharan kept secret from everyone that he himself was the father of the child.

The students of the hostel, where Phailna was a boarder, were greatly amused by Raicharan's country manners, and I have to confess that behind his father's back Phailna joined in their fun. But, in the bottom of their hearts, all the students loved the innocent and tender-hearted old man, and Phailna was very fond of him also. But, as I have said before, he loved him with a kind of condescension.

Raicharan grew older and older, and his employer was continually finding fault with him for his incompetent work. He had been starving himself for the boy's sake. So he had grown physically weak, and no longer up to his work. He would forget things, and his mind became dull and stupid. But his employer expected a full servant's work out of him, and would not brook excuses. The money that Raicharan had brought with him from the sale of his land was exhausted. The boy was continually grumbling about his clothes, and asking for more money.

Raicharan made up his mind. He gave up the situation where he was working as a servant, and left some money with Phailna and said, 'I have some business to do at home in my village, and will be back soon.'

He went off at once to Barasat where Anukul was the magistrate. Anukul's wife was still broken down with grief. She had had no other child.

One day Anukul was resting after a long and weary day in court. His wife was buying, at an exorbitant price, a herb from a mendicant quack, which was said to ensure the birth of a child. A voice of greeting was heard in the courtyard. Anukul went out to see who it was. It was Raicharan. Anukul's heart was softened when he saw his old servant. He asked him many questions, and offered to take him back into service.

Raicharan smiled faintly and said in reply, 'I want to make obeisance to my mistress.'

Anukul went with Raicharan into the house, where the mistress did not receive him as warmly as his old master. Raicharan took no notice of this, but folded his hands, and said, 'It was not the Padma that stole your baby. It was I.'

Anukul exclaimed, 'Great God! Eh! What! Where is he?' Raicharan replied, 'He is with me; I will bring him the day after tomorrow.'

It was Sunday. There was no magistrate's court sitting. Both husband and wife were looking expectantly along the road, waiting from early morning for Raicharan's appearance. At ten o'clock he came, leading Phailna by the hand.

Anukul's wife, without a question, took the boy into her lap, and was wild with excitement, sometimes laughing, sometimes weeping, touching him, kissing his hair and his forehead, and gazing into his face with hungry, eager eyes. The boy was very good-looking and dressed like a gentleman's son. The heart of Anukul brimmed over with a sudden rush of affection.

Nevertheless the magistrate in him asked, 'Have you any proof?'

Raicharan said, 'How could there be any proof of such a deed? God alone knows that I stole your boy, and no one else in the world.'

When Anukul saw how eagerly his wife was clinging to the boy, he realised the futility of asking for proof. It would be wiser to believe. And then, where could an old man like Raicharan get such a boy from? And why should his faithful servant deceive him for nothing?

'But,' he added severely, 'Raicharan, you must not stay here.'

'Where shall I go, Master?' said Raicharan, in a choking voice, folding his hands. 'I am old. Who will take in an old man as a servant?'

The mistress said, 'Let him stay. My child will be pleased. I forgive him.'

But Anukul's magisterial conscience would not allow him. 'No,' he said, 'he cannot be forgiven for what he has done.'

Raicharan bowed to the ground and clasped Anukul's feet. 'Master,' he cried, 'let me stay. It was not I who did it. It was God.'

Anukul's conscience was worse stricken than ever when Raicharan tried to put the blame on God's shoulders.

'No,' he said, 'I could not allow it. I cannot trust you any more. You have done an act of treachery.'

Raicharan rose to his feet and said, 'It was not I who did it.'

'Who was it then?' asked Anukul.

Raicharan replied, 'It was my fate.'

But no educated man could take this for an excuse. Anukul remained obdurate.

When Phailna saw that he was the wealthy magistrate's son, and not Raicharan's, he was angry at first, thinking that he had been cheated all this time of his birthright. But seeing Raicharan in distress, he generously said to his father, 'Father, forgive him. Even if you don't let him live with us, let him have a small monthly pension.'

After hearing this, Raicharan did not utter another word. He looked for the last time on the face of his son; he made obeisance to his old master and mistress. Then he went out and was mingled with the numberless people of the world.

At the end of the month Anukul sent him some money to his village. But the money came back. There was no one there of the name of Raicharan.

VISION

I

When I was a very young wife, I gave birth to a dead child and came near death myself. I recovered strength very slowly, and my eyesight became weaker and weaker.

My husband at this time was studying medicine. He was not altogether sorry to have a chance of testing his medical knowledge on me. So he began to treat my eyes himself.

My elder brother was reading for his law examination. One day he came to see me, and was alarmed at my condition.

'What are you doing?' he asked my husband. 'You are ruining Kumo's eyes. You ought to consult a good doctor at once.'

My husband said irritably, 'Why! What can a good doctor do more than I am doing? The case is quite a simple one, and the remedies are all well-known.'

Dada answered with scorn, 'I suppose you think there is no difference between you and a professor at Medical College.'

My husband replied angrily, 'If you ever get married, and there is a dispute about your wife's property, you won't take my advice about Law. Why, then, do you now come advising me about Medicine?'

While they were quarrelling, I was saying to myself that it was always the poor grass that suffered most when two kings went to war. Here was a dispute going on between these two, and I had to bear the brunt of it.

It also seemed to me very unfair that, when my family had given me in marriage, they should interfere afterwards. After all, my pleasure and pain are my husband's concern, not theirs.

From that day forward, merely over this trifling matter of my eyes, the bond between my husband and Dada was strained.

To my surprise, one afternoon, while my husband was away, Dada brought a doctor in to see me. He examined my eyes very carefully and looked grave. He said that further neglect would be dangerous. He wrote out a prescription for the medicine at once. When the strange doctor had gone, I implored my Dada not to interfere. I was sure that only evil would come from the stealthy visits of a doctor.

I was surprised at myself for plucking up courage to

speak to my brother like that. I had always hitherto been afraid of him. I am sure also that Dada was surprised at my boldness. He kept silence for a while, and then said to me, 'Very well, Kumo. I won't call in the doctor anymore. But when the medicine comes you must take it.'

Dada then went away. The medicine came from a chemist. I took it—bottles, powders, prescriptions and all—and threw it down the well!

My husband had been irritated by Dada's interference, and he began to treat my eyes with greater diligence than ever. He tried all sorts of remedies. I bandaged my eyes as he told me, I wore his coloured glasses, I put in his drops, I took all his powders. I even drank the cod liver oil he gave me.

Each time he came back from the hospital, he would ask me anxiously how I felt; and I would answer, 'Oh! Much better.' Indeed I became an expert in self-delusion. When I found that the water in my eyes was still increasing, I would console myself with the thought that it was a good thing to get rid of so much bad fluid, and when the flow of water in my eyes decreased, I was elated at my husband's skill.

But after a while the agony became unbearable. My eyesight faded away, and I had continual headaches day and night. I saw how much alarmed my husband was getting. I gathered from his manner that he was casting about for a pretext to call in a doctor. So I hinted that it might be as well to call one in.

I could see that he was greatly relieved. He called in an English doctor that very day. I do not know what talk they had together, but I gathered that the Sahib had spoken very sharply to my husband.

He remained silent for sometime after the doctor had gone. I took his hands in mine, and said, 'What an ill-mannered brute that was! Why didn't you call in an Indian doctor? That would have been much better. Do you think that man knows better than you do about my eyes?'

My husband was very silent for a moment, and then said with a broken voice, 'Kumo, your eyes must be operated on.'

I pretended to be vexed with him for concealing the fact from me so long.

'Here you have known this all the time,' said I, 'and yet you have said nothing about it! Do you think I am such a baby as to be afraid of an operation?'

At that he regained his good spirits. 'There are very few men,' said he, 'who are heroic enough to look forward to an operation without shrinking.'

I laughed at him. 'Yes, that is so. Men are heroic only before their wives!'

He looked at me gravely and said, 'You are perfectly right. We men are dreadfully vain.'

I laughed away his seriousness. 'Are you sure you can beat us women even in vanity?'

When Dada came, I took him aside. 'Dada, that treatment your doctor recommended would have done me a world of good. Unfortunately I mistook the mixture for the lotion. And since the day I made the mistake, my eyes have grown steadily worse; and now an operation is needed.'

Dada said to me, 'You were under your husband's treatment, and that is why I gave up coming to visit you.'

'No,' I answered. 'In reality, I was secretly treating myself in accordance with your doctor's directions.'

Oh! What lies we women have to tell! When we are mothers, we tell lies to pacify our children, and when we are wives, we tell lies to pacify the fathers of our children. We are never free from this necessity.

My deception had the effect of bringing about a better feeling between my husband and Dada. Dada blamed himself for asking me to keep a secret from my husband, and my husband regretted that he had not taken my brother's advice at first.

At last, with the consent of both, an English doctor came and operated on my left eye. That eye, however, was too weak to bear the strain; and the last flickering glimmer of light went out. Then the other eye gradually lost itself in darkness.

One day my husband came to my bedside. 'I cannot brazen it out before you any longer,' he said. 'Kumo, it is I who have ruined your eyes.'

I felt that his voice was choking with tears, so I took his right hand in both of mine and said, 'Why! You did exactly what was right. You have dealt only with that which was your very own. Just imagine, if some strange doctor had come and taken away my eyesight. What consolation should I have had then? But now I can feel that all has happened for the best and my great comfort is to know that it is at your hands I have lost my eyes. When Ramchandra found one lotus too few with which to worship God, he offered both his eyes in place of the lotus. And I have dedicated my eyes to my God. From now on, whenever you see something that is a joy to you, you must describe it to me and I will feed upon your words as a sacred gift left over from your vision.'

I do not mean, of course, that I said all this there and then, for it is impossible to speak these things on the spur of the moment. But I used to think over words like these for days and days together. And when I was very depressed, or if at any time the light of my devotion became dim, and I pitied my evil fate, then I made my mind utter these sentences, one by one, as a child repeats a story that is told. And so I could breathe once more the serener air of peace and love.

At the very time of our talk together, I said enough to show my husband what was in my heart.

'Kumo,' he said to me, 'the mischief I have done by my folly can never be made good. But I can do one thing. I can ever remain by your side, and try to make up for your want of vision as much as is in my power.'

'No,' said I. 'That will never do. I shall not ask you to turn your house into a hospital for the blind. There is only one thing to be done; you must marry again.'

As I tried to explain to him that this was necessary, my voice broke a little. I coughed, and tried to hide my emotion, but he burst out saying, 'Kumo, I know I am a fool, and a braggart, and all that, but I am not a villain! If ever I marry again, I swear to you—I swear to you the most solemn oath by my family god, Gopinath—may that most hated of all sins, the sin of parricide, fall on my head!'

Ah! I should never have allowed him to swear that dreadful oath. But tears were choking my voice, and I could not say a word for insufferable joy. I hid my blind face in my pillows and sobbed, and sobbed again. At last, when the first flood of my tears was over, I drew his head down to my breast.

'Ah!' I said, 'why did you take such a terrible oath? Do you think I asked you to marry again for your own sordid pleasure? No! I was thinking of myself, for she could perform those services which were mine to give you when I had my sight.'

'Services,' he said, 'services! Those can be done by servants. Do you think I am mad enough to bring a slave into my house, and bid her share the throne with my Goddess?'

As he said the word "Goddess", he held up my face in his hands and placed a kiss between my brows. At that moment the third eye of divine wisdom was opened, where he kissed me, and verily I had a consecration.

I said in my own mind, 'It is well. I am no longer able to serve him in the lower world of household cares. But I shall rise to a higher region. I shall bring down blessings from above. No more lies! No more deceptions for me! All the littlenesses and hypocrisies of my former life shall be banished forever!'

That day, the whole day through, I felt a conflict going on within me. The joy of the thought, that after this solemn oath it was impossible for my husband to marry again, fixed its roots deep in my heart, and I could not tear them out. But the new Goddess, who had taken her new throne in me, said, 'The time might come when it would be good for your husband to break his oath and marry again.' But the woman who was within me said, 'That may be; but all the same an oath is an oath, and there is no way out.'

The Goddess who was within me answered, 'That is no reason why you should exult over it.'

But the woman who was within me replied, 'What you say is quite true, no doubt; all the same he has taken his oath.' And the same story went on again and again. At last the Goddess frowned in silence, and the darkness of a horrible fear came down upon me.

My repentant husband would not let the servants do my work; he must do it all himself. At first it gave me unbounded delight to be dependent on him thus for every little thing. It was a means of keeping him by my side, and my desire to have him with me had become intense since my blindness. That share of his presence, which my eyes had lost, my other senses craved. When he was absent from my side, I would feel as if I were hanging in mid-air, and had lost my hold of all things tangible.

Formerly, when my husband came back late from the hospital, I used to open my window and gaze at the road. That road was the link which connected his world with mine. Now when I had lost that link through my blindness, all my body would go out to seek him. The bridge that united us had given way, and there was now this unsurpassable chasm. When he left my side the gulf seemed to yawn wide open. I could only wait for the time when he should cross back again from his own shore to mine.

But such intense longing and such utter dependence can never be good. A wife is a burden enough to a man, in all conscience, and to add to it the burden of this blindness was to make his life unbearable. I vowed that I would suffer alone, and never wrap my husband round in the folds of my all-pervading darkness.

Within an incredibly short space of time I managed to train myself to do all my household duties by the help of touch and sound and smell. In fact I soon found that I could get on with greater skill than before. For sight often distracts rather than helps us. And so it came to pass that, when these roving eyes of mine could do their work no longer, all the other senses took up their several duties with quietude and completeness.

When I gained experience by constant practice, I would not let my husband do any more household duties for me. He complained bitterly at first that I was depriving him of his penance.

This did not convince me. Whatever he might say, I could feel that he had a real sense of relief when these household duties were over. To serve daily a wife who is blind can never make up the life of a man.

II

My husband at last had finished his medical course. He went away from Calcutta to a small town to practise as a doctor. There in the country I felt with joy, through all my blindness, that I was restored to the arms of my mother. I had left my village birthplace for Calcutta when I was eight years old. Since then ten years had passed away, and in the great city the memory of my village home had grown dim. As long as I had eyesight, Calcutta with its busy life screened from view the memory of my early days. But when I lost my eyesight I knew for the first time that Calcutta allured only the eyes:

it could not fill the mind. And now, in my blindness, the scenes of my childhood shone out once more, like stars that appear one by one in the evening sky at the end of the day.

It was the beginning of November when we left Calcutta for Harsingpur. The place was new to me, but the scents and sounds of the countryside pressed round and embraced me. The morning breeze coming fresh from the newly ploughed land, the sweet and tender smell of the flowering mustard, the shepherd-boy's flute sounding in the distance, even the creaking noise of the bullock cart, as it groaned over the broken village road, filled my world with delight. The memory of my past life, with all its ineffable fragrance and sound, became a living present to me, and my blind eyes could not tell me I was wrong. I went back, and lived my childhood over again. Only one thing was absent: my mother was not with me.

I could see my home with the large peepul trees growing along the edge of the village pool. I could picture in my mind's eye my old grandmother seated on the ground with her thin wisps of hair untied, warming her back in the sun as she made the little round lentil balls to be dried and used for cooking. But somehow I could not recall the songs she used to croon to herself in her weak and quavering voice. In the evening, whenever I heard the lowing of cattle, I could almost watch the figure of my mother going round the sheds with a lighted lamp in her hand. The smell of the wet fodder and the pungent smoke of the straw fire would enter into my very heart. And in the distance I seemed to hear the clanging of the temple bell wafted up by the breeze from the river bank.

Calcutta, with all its turmoil and gossip, curdles the heart. There all the beautiful duties of life lose their freshness and innocence. I remember one day, when a friend of mine came in and said to me, 'Kumo, why don't you feel angry? If I had been treated like you by my husband, I would never look upon his face again.'

She tried to make me indignant, because he had been so long in calling a doctor.

'My blindness,' said I, 'was itself a sufficient evil. Why should I make it worse by allowing hatred to grow against my husband?'

My friend shook her head in great contempt when she heard such old-fashioned talk from the lips of a mere chit of a girl. She went away in disdain. But whatever might be my answer at the time, such words as these left their poison; and the venom was never wholly got out of the soul when once the words had been uttered.

So you see, Calcutta, with its never-ending gossip, does harden the heart. But when I came back to the country, all my earlier hopes and faiths, all that I held true in life during childhood became fresh and bright once more. God came to me and filled my heart and my world. I bowed to Him and said, 'It is well that You have taken away my eyes. You are with me.'

Ah! But I said more than was right. It was a presumption to say, 'You are with me.' All we can say is this, 'I must be true to You.' Even when nothing is left for us, we still have to go on living.

III

We passed a few happy months together. My husband gained some reputation in his profession as a doctor. And money came with it.

But there is a mischief in money. I cannot point to any one event; but, because the blind have keener perceptions than other people, I could discern the change which came over my husband along with the increase of wealth.

He had a keen sense of justice when he was younger, and had often told me of his great desire to help the poor when once he obtained a practice of his own. He had a noble contempt for those in his profession who would not feel the pulse of a poor patient before collecting his fee. But now I noticed a difference. He had become strangely hard. Once when a poor woman came, and begged him, out of charity, to save the life of her only child, he bluntly refused. And when I implored him myself to help her, he did his work perfunctorily.

When we had been less rich, my husband disliked sharp practice in money matters. He was scrupulously honourable in such things. But since he had got a large account at the bank he was often closeted for hours with some scamp of a landlord's agent, for purposes which clearly boded no good.

Where has he drifted? What has become of this husband of mine—the husband I knew before I was blind; the husband who kissed me that day between my brows, and enshrined me on the throne of a Goddess? Those whom a sudden gust of passion brings down to the dust can rise up again with a new strong impulse of goodness. But those who, day by day, become dried up in the very fibre of their moral being; those who, by some outer parasitic growth, choke the inner life by slow degrees—such wench one day a deadness which knows no healing.

The separation caused by blindness is the merest physical trifle. But ah! It suffocates me to find that he is no longer with me, where he stood with me in that hour when we both knew that I was blind. That is a separation indeed!

I, with my love fresh and my faith unbroken, have kept to the shelter of my heart's inner shrine. But my husband has left the cool shade of those things that are ageless and unfading. He is fast disappearing into the barren, waterless waste in his mad thirst for gold.

Sometimes the suspicion comes to me that things are not so bad as they seem: that perhaps I exaggerate because

I am blind. It may be that, if my eyesight were unimpaired, I should have accepted the world as I found it. This, at any rate, was the light in which my husband looked at all my moods and fancies.

One day an old Musalman came to the house. He asked my husband to visit his little granddaughter. I could hear the old man say, 'Baba, I am a poor man; but come with me, and Allah will do you good.' My husband answered coldly, 'What Allah will do won't help matters; I want to know what you can do for me.'

When I heard it, I wondered in my mind why God had not made me deaf as well as blind. The old man heaved a deep sigh and departed. I sent my maid to fetch him to my room. I met him at the door of the inner apartment and put some money into his hand.

'Please take this from me,' said I, 'for your little granddaughter, and get a trustworthy doctor to look after her. And … pray for my husband.'

But the whole of that day I could take no food at all. In the afternoon, when my husband got up from sleep, he asked me, 'Why do you look so pale?'

I was about to say, as I used to do in the past, 'Oh! It's nothing,' but those days of deception were over, and I spoke to him plainly.

'I have been hesitating,' I said, 'for days altogether, to tell you something. It has been hard to think what exactly it was I wanted to say. Even now I may not be able to explain what I had in my mind. But I am sure you know what has happened. Our lives have drifted apart.'

My husband laughed in a forced manner, and said, 'Change is the law of nature.'

I said to him, 'I know that. But there are some things that are eternal.'

Then he became serious.

'There are many women,' said he, 'who have a real cause for sorrow. There are some whose husbands do not earn money. There are others whose husbands do not love them. But you are making yourself wretched about nothing at all.'

Then it became clear to me that my very blindness had conferred on me the power of seeing a world which is beyond all change. Yes! It is true. I am not like other women. And my husband will never understand me.

IV

Our two lives went on with their dull routine for some time. Then there was a break in the monotony. An aunt of my husband came to pay us a visit.

The first thing she blurted out after our first greeting was this, 'Well, Krum, it's a great pity you have become blind; but why do you impose your own affliction on your husband? You must get him to another wife.'

There was an awkward pause. If my husband had only said something in jest, or laughed in her face, all would have been over. But he stammered and hesitated, and said at last in a nervous, stupid way, 'Do you really think so? Really, Aunt, you shouldn't talk like that.'

His aunt appealed to me. 'Was I wrong, Kumo?'

I laughed a hollow laugh.

'Had not you better,' said I, 'consult someone more competent to decide? The pickpocket never asks permission from the man whose pocket he is going to pick.'

'You are quite right,' she replied blandly. 'Abinash, my dear, let us have our little conference in private. What do you say to that?'

After a few days my husband asked her in my presence if she knew of any girl of a decent family who could come and help me in my household work. He knew quite well that I needed no help. I kept silent.

'Oh! There are heaps of them,' replied his aunt. 'My cousin has a daughter who is just of marriageable age, and as nice a girl as you could wish. Her people would be only too glad to secure you as a husband.'

Again there came from him that forced, hesitating laugh, and he said, 'But I never mentioned marriage.'

'How could you expect,' asked his aunt, 'a girl of decent family to come and live in your house without marriage?'

He had to admit that this was reasonable, and remained nervously silent.

I stood alone within the closed doors of my blindness after he had gone, and called upon my God and prayed, 'O God, save my husband.'

When I was coming out of the household shrine from my morning worship a few days later, his aunt took hold of both my hands warmly.

'Kumo, here is the girl,' said she, 'we were speaking about the other day. Her name is Hemangini. She will be delighted to meet you. Hemo, come here and be introduced to your sister.'

My husband entered the room at the same moment. He feigned surprise when he saw the strange girl, and was about to retire. But his aunt said, 'Abinash, my dear, what are you running away for? There is no need to do that. Here is my cousin's daughter, Hemangini, come to see you. Hemo, make your bow to him.'

As if taken quite by surprise, he began to ply his aunt with questions about the when and why and how of the new arrival.

I saw the hollowness of the whole thing, and took Hemangini by the hand and led her to my own room. I gently stroked her face and arms and hair, and found that she was about fifteen years old, and very beautiful.

As I felt her face, she suddenly burst out laughing and

said, 'Why! What are you doing? Are you hypnotising me?'

That sweet ringing laughter of hers swept away in a moment all the dark clouds that stood between us. I threw my right arm about her neck.

'Dear one,' I said, 'I am trying to see you.' And again I stroked her soft face with my left hand.

'Trying to see me?' she said, with a new burst of laughter. 'Am I like a vegetable marrow, grown in your garden, that you want to feel me all round to see how soft I am?'

I suddenly realised that she did not know I had lost my sight.

'Sister, I am blind,' said I.

She was silent. I could feel her big young eyes, full of curiosity, peering into my face. I knew they were full of pity. Then she grew thoughtful and puzzled, and said, after a short pause, 'Oh! I see now. That was the reason your husband invited his aunt to come and stay here.'

'No!' I replied, 'you are quite mistaken. He did not ask her to come. She came of her own accord.'

Hemangini went off into a peal of laughter. 'That's just like my aunt,' said she. 'Oh, wasn't it nice of her to come without any invitation? But now that she's come, you won't get her to move for some time, I can assure you!'

Then she paused, and looked puzzled.

'But why did father send me?' she asked. 'Can you tell me that?'

The aunt had come into the room while we were talking. Hemangini said to her, 'When are you thinking of going back, Aunt?'

The aunt looked very much upset.

'What a question to ask!' she said. 'I've never seen such a restless body as you. We've only just come, and you ask when we're going back!'

'It is all very well for you,' Hemangini said, 'for this house belongs to your near relations. But what about me? I tell you plainly I can't stop here.' And then she held my hand and said, 'What do you think, dear?'

I drew her to my heart, but said nothing. The aunt was in a great difficulty. She felt the situation was getting beyond her control; so she proposed that she and her niece should go out together to bathe.

'No! We two will go together,' said Hemangini, clinging to me. The aunt gave in, fearing opposition if she tried to drag her away.

Going down to the river, Hemangini asked me, 'Why don't you have children?'

I was startled by her question, and answered, 'How can I tell? My God has not given me any. That is the reason.'

'No! That's not the reason,' said Hemangini quickly. 'You must have committed some sin. Look at my aunt. She is childless. It must be because her heart has some wickedness. But what wickedness is in your heart?'

The words hurt me. I have no solution to offer for the problem of evil. I sighed deeply, and said in the silence of my soul, 'My God! You know the reason.'

'Gracious goodness,' cried Hemangini, 'what are you sighing for? No one ever takes me seriously.'

And her laughter pealed across the river.

V

I found out after this that there were constant interruptions in my husband's professional duties. He refused all calls from a distance, and would hurry away from his patients, even when they were close at hand.

Formerly it was only during the mid-day meals and at nighttime that he could come into the inner apartment. But now, with unnecessary anxiety for his aunt's comfort, he began to visit her at all hours of the day. I knew at once that he had come to her room when I heard her shouting for Hemangini to bring in a glass of water. At first the girl would do what she was told; but later on she refused altogether.

Then the aunt would call, in an endearing voice, 'Hemo! Hemo! Hemangini?' But the girl would cling to me with an impulse of pity. A sense of dread and sadness would keep her silent. Sometimes she would shrink towards me like a hunted thing who scarcely knew what was coming.

About this time my brother came down from Calcutta to visit me. I knew how keen his powers of observation were, and what a hard judge he was. I feared my husband would be put on his defence, and have to stand his trial before him. So I endeavoured to hide the true situation behind a mask of noisy cheerfulness. But I am afraid I overdid the part; it was unnatural for me.

My husband began to fidget openly, and asked how long my brother was going to stay. At last his impatience became little short of insulting, and my brother had no help for it but to leave. Before going, he placed his hand on my head and kept it there for sometime. I noticed that his hand shook, and a tear fell from his eyes, as he silently gave me his blessing.

I well remember that it was an evening in April, and a market-day. People who had come into town were going back home from market. There was the feeling of an impending storm in the air; the smell of the wet earth and the moisture in the wind were all-pervading. I never keep a lighted lamp in my bedroom when I am alone, lest my clothes should catch fire, or some accident happen. I sat on the floor in my dark room and called upon the God of my blind world.

'O my Lord,' I cried, 'Your face is hidden. I cannot see. I am blind. I hold tight this broken rudder of a heart till my hands bleed. The waves have become too strong for me. How long will you try me, my God, how long?'

I kept my head prone upon the bedstead and began to sob. As I did so, I felt the bedstead move a little. The next moment Hemangini was by my side. She clung to my neck and wiped my tears away silently. I do not know why she had been waiting that evening in the inner room, or why she had been lying alone there in the dusk. She asked me no question. She said no word. She simply placed her cool hand on my forehead, and kissed me, and departed.

The next morning Hemangini said to her aunt in my presence, 'If you want to stay on, you can. But I don't. I'm going home with our family servant.'

The aunt said there was no need for her to go alone, for she was going away also. Then smilingly and mincingly she brought out, from a plush case, a ring set with pearls.

'Look, Hemo,' she said, 'what a beautiful ring my Abinash brought for you.'

Hemangini snatched the ring from her hand.

'Look, Aunt,' she answered quickly, 'just see how splendidly I aim.' And she flung the ring into the tank outside the window.

The aunt, overwhelmed with alarm, vexation and surprise, bristled like a hedgehog. She turned to me, and held me by the hand.

'Kumo,' she repeated again and again, 'don't say a word about this childish freak to Abinash. He would be fearfully vexed.'

I assured her that she need not fear. Not a word would reach him about it from my lips.

The next day before starting for home Hemangini embraced me, and said, 'Dearest, keep me in mind; do not forget me.'

I stroked her face over and over with my fingers, and said, 'Sister, the blind have long memories.'

I drew her head towards me and kissed her hair and her forehead. My world suddenly became grey. All the beauty and laughter and tender youth, which had nestled so close to me, vanished when Hemangini departed. I went groping about with arms outstretched, seeking to find out what was left in my deserted world.

My husband came in later. He affected a great relief now that they were gone, but it was exaggerated and empty. He pretended that his aunt's visit had kept him away from work.

Hitherto there had been only the one barrier of blindness between me and my husband. Now another barrier was added—this deliberate silence about Hemangini. He feigned utter indifference, but I knew he was having letters about her.

It was early in May. My maid entered my room one morning, and asked me, 'What is all this preparation going on at the landing on the river? Where is Master going?'

I knew there was something impending, but I said to the maid, 'I can't say.'

The maid did not dare to ask me any more questions. She sighed, and went away.

Late that night my husband came to me.

'I have to visit a patient in the country,' said he. 'I shall have to start very early tomorrow morning, and I may have to be away for two or three days.'

I got up from my bed. I stood before him and cried aloud, 'Why are you telling me lies?'

My husband stammered, 'What—what lies have I told you?'

I said, 'You are going to get married.'

He remained silent. For some moments there was no sound in the room. Then I broke the silence. 'Answer me,' I cried. 'Say yes.'

He answered, 'Yes,' like a feeble echo.

I shouted out with a loud voice, 'No! I shall never allow you. I shall save you from this great disaster, this dreadful sin. If I fail in this, then why am I your wife, and why did I ever worship my God?'

The room remained still as a stone. I dropped on the floor and clung to my husband's knees.

'What have I done?' I asked. 'Where have I been lacking? Tell me truly. Why do you want another wife?'

My husband said slowly, 'I will tell you the truth. I am afraid of you. Your blindness has enclosed you in its fortress, and I have now no entrance. To me you are no longer a woman. You are as awful as my God. I cannot live my everyday life with you. I want a woman—just an ordinary woman—whom I can be free to chide and coax and pet and scold.'

Oh, tear open my heart and see! What am I other than that—just an ordinary woman? I am the same girl that I was when I was newly wed, a girl with all her need to believe, to confide, to worship.

I do not recollect exactly the words that I uttered. I only remember that I said, 'If I be a true wife, then, may God be my witness, you shall never do this wicked deed, you shall never break your oath. Before you commit such sacrilege, either I shall become a widow, or Hemangini shall die.'

Then I fell down on the floor in a swoon. When I came to myself, it was still dark. The birds were silent. My husband had gone.

All that day I sat at my worship in the sanctuary at the household shrine. In the evening a fierce storm, with thunder and lightning and rain, swept down upon the house and shook it. As I crouched before the shrine, I did not ask my God to save my husband from the storm, though he must have been at that time in peril on the river. I prayed that whatever might happen to me, my husband might be saved from this great sin.

Night passed. The whole of the next day I kept my seat

at worship. When it was evening there was the noise of shaking and beating at the door. When the door was broken open, they found me lying unconscious on the ground, and carried me to my room.

When I came to myself at last, I heard someone whispering in my ear, 'Sister.'

I found that I was lying in my room with my head on Hemangini's lap. When my head moved, I heard her dress rustle. It was the sound of bridal silk.

O my God, my God! My prayer has gone unheeded! My husband has fallen!

Hemangini bent her head low, and said in a sweet whisper, 'Sister, dearest, I have come to ask your blessing on our marriage.'

At first my whole body stiffened like the trunk of a tree that has been struck by lightning. Then I sat up, and said, painfully, forcing myself to speak the words, 'Why should I not bless you? You have done no wrong.'

Hemangini laughed her merry laugh.

'Wrong!' said she. 'When you married, it was right; and when I marry, you call it wrong!'

I tried to smile in answer to her laughter. I said in my mind, 'My prayer is not the final thing in this world. His will is all. Let the blows descend upon my head; but may they leave my faith and hope in God untouched.'

Hemangini bowed to me and touched my feet. 'May

you be happy,' said I, blessing her, 'and enjoy unbroken prosperity.'

Hemangini was still unsatisfied.

'Dearest sister,' she said, 'a blessing for me is not enough. You must make our happiness complete. You must, with those saintly hands of yours, accept into your home my husband also. Let me bring him to you.'

I said, 'Yes, bring him to me.'

A few moments later I heard a familiar footstep, and the question, 'Kumo, how are you?'

I started up, and bowed to the ground, and cried, 'Dada!'

Hemangini burst out laughing.

'You still call him elder brother?' she asked. 'What nonsense! Call him younger brother now, and pull his ears and tease him, for he has married me, your younger sister.'

Then I understood. My husband had been saved from that great sin. He had not fallen.

I knew my Dada had determined never to marry. And, since my mother had died, there was no sacred wish of hers to implore him to wedlock. But I, his sister, by my sore need had brought it to pass. He had married for my sake.

Tears of joy gushed from my eyes, and poured down my cheeks. I tried, but I could not stop them. Dada slowly passed his fingers through my hair. Hemangini clung to me, and went on laughing.

I was lying awake in my bed for the best part of the night, waiting with straining anxiety for my husband's return. I could not imagine how he would bear the shock of shame and disappointment.

When it was long past the hour of midnight, slowly my door opened. I sat up on my bed and listened. They were the footsteps of my husband. My heart began to beat wildly. He came up to my bed and held my hand in his.

'Your Dada,' said he, 'has saved me from destruction. I was being dragged down by a moment's madness. An infatuation had seized me, from which I seemed unable to escape. God alone knows what a load I was carrying on that day when I entered the boat. The storm came down on the river and covered the sky. In the midst of all fears I had a secret wish in my heart to be drowned, and so disentangle my life from the knot which I had tied it. I reached Mathurganj. There I heard the news which set me free. Your brother had married Hemangini. I cannot tell you with what joy and shame I heard it. I hastened on board the boat again. In that moment of self-revelation I knew that I could have no happiness except with you. You are a Goddess.'

I laughed and cried at the same time, and said, 'No, no, no! I am not going to be a Goddess any longer. I am simply your own little wife. I am an ordinary woman.'

'Dearest,' he replied, 'There is also something I want to

say to you. Never again put me to shame by calling me your God.'

On the next day the little town became joyous with the sound of conch shells. But nobody spoke again about that night of madness, when all was so nearly lost.

LIVING OR DEAD?

I

The widow in the house of Saradasankar, the Ranihat zamindar, had no relative on her father's side of the family. One after the other all had died. Nor had she in her husband's family anyone she could call her own—neither husband nor son. The child of her brother-in-law Saradasankar was her darling. For a long time after his birth, his mother had been very ill, and the widow, his aunt Kadambini, had fostered him. If a woman fosters another's child, her love for him is all the stronger because she has no claim upon him—no claim of kinship, that is, but simply the claim of love. Love cannot prove its claim by any document which society accepts, and does not wish to prove it; it merely worships with double passion its life's uncertain treasure. Thus all the widow's thwarted love went out towards this little child. One night in the month of Sraban, Kadambini died suddenly. For some reason her heart stopped beating. Everywhere else the world held on its course; only in this gentle little breast, suffering with love, the watch of time stood still forever.

Four of the zamindar's Brahmin servants took away the body, without ceremony, to be burned. The burning ground of Ranihat was very far from the village. There was a hut beside a tank, a huge banyan tree near it, and nothing more. Formerly what used to be a river, now completely dried up, ran through the ground, and part of the watercourse had been dug out to make a tank for the performance of funeral rites. The people considered the tank as part of the river and reverenced it as such.

Taking the body into the hut, the four men sat down to wait for the wood. The time seemed so long that two of the four grew restless, and went to see why it did not come. Nitai and Gurucharan being gone, Bidhu and Banamali remained to watch over the body.

It was a dark night of Sraban. Heavy clouds hung in a starless sky. The two men sat silent in the dark room. Their matches and lamp were useless. The matches were damp, and would not light, for all their efforts, and the lantern went out.

After a long silence, one said, 'Brother, it would be good if we had a bowl of tobacco. In our hurry we brought none.'

The other answered, 'I can run and bring all we want.'

Understanding why Banamali wanted to go (for fear of ghosts, the burning ground being considered haunted), Bidhu said, 'I daresay! Meanwhile, I suppose I am to sit here alone!'

Conversation ceased again. Five minutes seemed like an hour. In their minds they cursed the two who had gone to fetch the wood, and they began to suspect that they sat gossiping in some pleasant nook. There was no sound anywhere, except the incessant noise of frogs and crickets from the tank. Then suddenly they fancied that the bed shook slightly, as if the dead body had turned on its side. Bidhu and Banamali trembled, and began muttering, 'Ram, Ram.' A deep sigh was heard in the room. In a moment the watchers leapt out of the hut and raced for the village.

After running about three miles, they met their colleagues coming back with a lantern. As a matter of fact, they had gone to smoke, and knew nothing about the wood. But they declared that a tree had been cut down, and that, when it was split up, it would be brought along at once. Then Bidhu and Banamali told them what had happened in the hut. Nitai and Gurucharan scoffed at the story, and abused Bidhu and Banamali angrily for leaving their duty.

Without delay, all four returned to the hut. As they entered, they saw at once that the body was gone; nothing but an empty bed remained. They stared at one another. Could a jackal have taken it? But there was no scrap of clothing anywhere. Going outside, they saw that on the mud they had collected at the door of the hut there were a woman's tiny footprints, newly made. They knew that Saradasankar was no fool, and they could hardly persuade him to believe in this ghost story. So, after much discussion the four decided that it would be best to say that the body had been burnt.

Towards dawn, when the men with the wood arrived, they were told that, owing to their delay, the work had been done without them; there had been some wood in the hut after all. No one was likely to question this, since a dead body is not such a valuable property that anyone would steal it.

II

Every one knows that, even when there is no sign, life is often secretly present, and may begin again in an apparently dead body. Kadambini was not dead; only the machine of her life had for some reason suddenly stopped.

When consciousness returned, she saw dense darkness on all sides. It occurred to her that she was not lying in her usual place. She called out 'Sister,' but no answer came from the darkness. As she sat up, terror-stricken, she remembered her death bed, the sudden pain at her breast, the beginning of a choking sensation. Her elder sister-in-law was warming some milk for the child when Kadambini became faint, and fell on the bed, saying with a choking voice, 'Sister, bring the child here. I am worried.' After that, everything was black, as when an inkpot is upset over an exercise book. Kadambini's memory and consciousness, all the letters of the world's book, in a moment became formless. The widow could not remember whether the child, in the sweet voice of love, called her 'Auntie,' as if for the last time, or not; she could not remember whether, as she left the world, she knew death's endless unknown journey, she had received a parting gift of affection, love's passage-money for the silent land. At first, I fancy, she thought the lonely dark place was the House of Yama, where there is nothing to see, nothing to hear, nothing to do, only an eternal watch. But when a cold damp wind drove through the open door, and she heard the croaking of frogs, she remembered vividly and in a moment all the rains of her short life, and could feel her kinship with the earth. Then came a flash of lightning, and she saw the tank, the banyan, the great plain, the far-off trees. She remembered how at full moon she had sometimes come to bathe in this tank, and how dreadful death had seemed when she had seen a corpse on the burning ground.

Her first thought was to return home. But then she reflected, 'I am dead. How can I return home? That would bring disaster on them. I have left the kingdom of the living; I am my own ghost!' If this were not so, she reasoned, how could she have got out of Saradasankar's well-guarded zenana, and come to this distant burning ground at midnight? Also, if her funeral rites had not been finished, where had the men gone who should burn her? Recalling her death-moment in Saradasankar's brightly-lit house, she now found herself alone in a distant, deserted, dark burning ground. Surely she was no member of earthly society! Surely she was a creature of horror, of ill-omen, her own ghost!

At this thought, all the bonds were snapped which bound her to the world. She felt that she had marvellous strength, endless freedom. She could do what she liked, go where she pleased. Mad with the inspiration of this new idea, she rushed from the hut like a gust of wind and stood upon the burning ground. All trace of shame or fear had left her.

But as she walked on and on, her feet grew tired, her body weak. The plain stretched on endlessly. There were paddy fields here and there and sometimes she found herself standing knee-deep in water.

At the first glimmer of dawn she heard one or two birds cry from the bamboo-clumps by the distant houses. Then terror seized her. She could not tell in what new relation she stood to the earth and to living folk. As long as she had been on the plain, on the burning-ground, covered by the dark night of Sraban, so long she had been fearless, a denizen of her own kingdom. By daylight the homes of men filled her with fear. Men and ghosts dread each other, for their tribes inhabit different banks of the river of death.

III

Her clothes were clotted in the mud; strange thoughts and walking by night had given her the aspect of a madwoman; truly, her apparition was such that folk might have been afraid of her, and children might have stoned her or run away. Luckily, the first to catch sight of her was a traveller. He came up and said, 'Mother, you look like a respectable woman. Wherever are you going, alone and in this guise?'

Kadambini, unable to collect her thoughts, stared at him in silence. She could not think that she was still in touch with the world, that she looked like a respectable woman, that a traveller was asking her questions.

Again the man said, 'Come, mother, I will see you home. Tell me where you live.'

Kadambini thought. To return to her father-in-law's house would be absurd, and she had no father's house. Then she remembered the friend of her childhood. She had not seen Jogmaya since the days of her youth, but from time to time they had exchanged letters. Occasionally there had been quarrels between them, as was only right, since Kadambini wished to make it clear that her love for Jogmaya was unbounded, while her friend complained that Kadambini did not return a love equal to her own. They were both sure that, if they once met, they would be inseparable.

Kadambini said to the traveller, 'I will go to Sripati's house at Nisindapur.'

As he was going to Calcutta, Nisindapur, though not near, was on his way. So he took Kadambini to Sripati s house, and the friends met again. At first they did not recognise one another, but gradually each recognised the features of the other's childhood.

'What luck!' said Jogmaya. 'I never dreamt that I should see you again. But how have you come here, sister? Your father-in-law's folk surely didn't let you go!'

Kadambini remained silent, and at last said, 'Sister, do not ask about my father-in-law. Give me a corner, and treat me as a servant. I will do your work.'

'What?' cried Jogmaya. 'Keep you like a servant! Why, you are my closest friend, you are my—' and so on.

Just then Sripati came in. Kadambini stared at him for sometime, and then went out very slowly. She kept her head uncovered, and showed not the slightest modesty or respect. Jogmaya, fearing that Sripati would be prejudiced against her friend, began an elaborate explanation. But Sripati, who readily agreed to anything Jogmaya said, cut short her story, and left his wife uneasy in her mind.

Kadambini had come, but she was not the same person her friend had thought she was: death was between them. She could feel no intimacy for others so long as her existence perplexed her and consciousness remained. Kadambini would look at Jogmaya and brood. She would think, 'She has her husband and her work, she lives in a world far away from mine. She shares affection and duty with the people of the world; I am an empty shadow. She is among the living, and I am in eternity.'

Jogmaya also was uneasy, but could not explain why. Women do not love mystery, because, though uncertainty may be transmuted into poetry, into heroism, into scholarship, it cannot be turned to account in household work. So, when a woman cannot understand a thing, she either destroys and forgets it or shapes it anew for her own use. If she fails to deal with it in one of these ways, she loses her temper with it. The greater Kadambini's abstraction became, the more impatient was Jogmaya with her, wondering what trouble weighed upon her mind.

Then a new danger arose. Kadambini was afraid of herself; yet she could not flee from herself. Those who fear ghosts fear those who are behind them; wherever they cannot see, there is fear. But Kadambini's chief terror lay in herself, for she dreaded nothing external. At the dead of night, when alone in her room, she screamed; in the evening, when she saw her shadow in the lamp light, her whole body shook. Watching her fearfulness, the rest of the house fell into a sort of terror. The servants and Jogmaya herself began to see ghosts.

One midnight, Kadambini came out of her bedroom,

weeping, and wailed at Jogmaya's door, 'Sister, sister, let me lie at your feet! Do not put me by myself!'

Jogmaya's anger was no less than her fear. She would have liked to drive Kadambini from the house that very second. The good-natured Sripati, after much effort, succeeded in quieting their guest, and put her in the next room.

Next day Sripati was unexpectedly summoned to his wife's apartments. She began to upbraid him. 'You, do you call yourself a man? A woman runs away from her father-in-law and enters your house; a month passes, and you haven't hinted that she should go away, nor have I heard the slightest protest from you. I should take it as a favour if you would explain yourself. You men are all alike.'

Men, as a race, have a natural partiality for womankind in general, foe which women themselves hold them accountable. Although Sripati was prepared to touch Jogmaya's body, and swear that his kind feeling towards the helpless but beautiful Kadambini was no whit greater than it should be, he could not prove it by his behaviour. He thought that her father-in-law's people must have treated this forlorn widow abominably, if she could bear it no longer, and was driven to take refuge with him. As she had neither father nor mother, how could he desert her? So saying, he let the matter drop, for he had no mind to distress Kadambini by asking her unpleasant questions.

His wife, then, tried other means of her sluggish lord, until at last he saw that for the sake of peace he must send word to Kadambini's father-in-law. The result of a letter, he thought, might not be satisfactory; so he resolved to go to Ranihat, and act on what he learnt.

So Sripati went, and Jogmaya on her part, said to Kadambini, 'Friend, it hardly seems proper for you to stop here any longer. What will people say?'

Kadambini stared solemnly at Jogmaya, and said, 'What have I to do with people?'

Jogmaya was astounded. Then she said sharply, 'If you have nothing to do with people, we have. How can we explain the detention of a woman belonging to another house?'

Kadambini said, 'Where is my father-in-law's house?'

'Confound it!' thought Jogmaya. 'What will the wretched woman say next?'

Very slowly, Kadambini said, 'What have I to do with you? Am I of the earth? You laugh, weep, love; each grips and holds his own; I merely look. You are human, I a shadow. I cannot understand why God has kept me in this world of yours.'

So strange were her look and speech that Jogmaya understood something of her drift, though not all. Unable either to dismiss her, or to ask her any more questions, she went away, oppressed with thought.

IV

It was nearly ten o'clock at night when Sripati returned from Ranihat. The earth was drowned in torrents of rain. It seemed that the downpour would never stop, that the night would never end.

Jogmaya asked, 'Well?'

'I've lots to say, presently.'

So saying, Sripati changed his clothes and sat down to supper; then he lay dawn for a smoke. His mind was perplexed.

His wife stilled her curiosity for a long time; then she came to his couch and demanded, 'What did you hear?'

'That you have certainly made a mistake.'

Jogmaya was nettled. Women never make mistakes, or, if they do, a sensible man never mentions them; it is better to take them on his own shoulders. Jogmaya snapped, 'May I be permitted to hear how?'

Sripati replied, 'The woman you have taken into your house is not your Kadambini.'

Hearing this, she was greatly annoyed, especially since it was her husband who said it. 'What! I don't know my own friend? I must come to you to recognise her! You are clever indeed!'

Sripati explained that there was no need to quarrel about his cleverness. He could prove what he said. There was no doubt that Jogmaya's Kadambini was dead.

Jogmaya replied, 'Listen! You've certainly made some huge mistake. You've been to the wrong house, or are confused as to what you have heard. Who told you to go yourself? Write a letter, and everything will be cleared up.'

Sripati was hurt by his wife's lack of faith in his executive ability; he produced all sorts of proof, without result. Midnight found them still asserting and contradicting. They were both agreed now that Kadambini should be got out of the house, and Sripati believed that their guest had deceived his wife all the time by a pretended acquaintance. Jogmaya thought that she was a prostitute, yet in the present discussion neither would acknowledge defeat. By degrees their voices became so loud that they forgot that Kadambini was sleeping in the next room.

The one said, 'We're in a nice fix! I tell you, I heard it with my own ears!' And the other answered angrily, 'What do I care about that? I can see with my own eyes surely.'

At length Jogmaya said, 'Very well. Tell me when Kadambini died.' She thought that if she could find a discrepancy between the day of death and the date of some letter from Kadambini, she could prove that Sripati erred.

He told her the date of Kadambini's death, and they both saw that it fell on the very day before she came to their house. Jogmaya's heart trembled; even Sripati was not unmoved.

Just then the door flew open; a damp wind swept in and blew the lamp out. The darkness rushed after it, and filled the whole house. Kadambini stood in the room. It was nearly one o'clock, the rain was pelting outside.

Kadambini spoke, 'Friend, I am your Kadambini, but I am no longer living. I am dead.'

Jogmaya screamed with terror; Sripati could not speak.

'But, save in being dead, I have done you no wrong. If I have no place among the living, I have none among the dead. Oh! Whither shall I go?'

Crying as if to wake the sleeping Creator in the dense night of rain, she asked again, 'Oh! Whither shall I go?'

So saying, Kadambini left her friend fainting in the dark house and went out into the world, seeking her own place.

V

It is hard to say how Kadambini reached Ranihat. At first she showed herself to no one, but spent the whole day in a ruined temple, starving. When the untimely afternoon of the rains was pitch-black, and people huddled in their houses for fear of the impending storm, then Kadambini came forth. Her heart trembled as she reached her father-in-law's house; and when, drawing a thick veil over her face, she entered, none of the doorkeepers objected, since they took her for a servant. And the rain was pouring down, and the wind howled.

The mistress, Saradasankar's wife, was playing cards with her widowed sister. A servant was in the kitchen, the sick child was sleeping in the bedroom. Kadambini, escaping every one's notice, entered this room. I do not know why she had come to her father-in-law's house; she herself did not know; she felt only that she wanted to see her child again. She had no thought where to go next, or what to do.

In the lighted room she saw the child sleeping, his fists clenched, his body wasted with fever. At the sight of him, her heart became parched and thirsty. If only she could press that tortured body to her breast! Immediately the thought followed, 'I do not exist. Who would see it? His mother loves company, gossip and cards. All the time that she left me in charge, she was herself free from anxiety, nor was she troubled about him in the least. Who will look after him now as I did?'

The child turned on his side and cried, half asleep, 'Auntie, give me water.' Her darling had not yet forgotten his auntie! In a fever of excitement, she poured out some water, and, taking him to her breast, she gave it to him.

As long as he was asleep, the child felt no strangeness in taking water from the accustomed hand. But when Kadambini satisfied her long-starved longing, and kissed him and began rocking him asleep again, he awoke and embraced her. 'Did you die, Auntie?' he asked.

'Yes, darling.'

'And you have come back? Do not die again.'

Before she could answer, disaster overtook her. One of

the maidservants coming in with a cup of sago dropped it, and fell down. At the crash the mistress left her cards and entered the room. She stood like a pillar of wood, unable to flee or speak. Seeing all this, the child, too, became terrified, and burst out weeping, 'Go away, Auntie,' he said, 'go away!'

Now at last Kadambini understood that she had not died. The old room, the old things, the same child, the same love, all returned to their living state, without change or difference between her and them. In her friend's house she had felt that her childhood's companion was dead. In her child's room she knew that the boy's Auntie was not dead at all. In anguished tones she said, 'Sister, why do you dread me? See, I am as you knew me.'

Her sister-in-law could endure no longer, and fell into a faint. Saradasankar himself entered the zenana. With folded hands, he said piteously, 'Is this right? Satis is my only son. Why do you show yourself to him? Are we not your own kin? Since you went, he has wasted away daily. His fever has been incessant; day and night he cries, "Auntie, Auntie". You have left the world; break these bonds of maya. We will perform all funeral honours.'

Kadambini could bear no more. She said, 'Oh, I am not dead, I am not dead. Oh, how can I persuade you that I am not dead? I am living, living!' She lifted a brass pot from the ground and dashed it against her forehead. The blood ran from her brow. 'Look!' she cried, 'I am living!' Saradasankar stood like an image; the child screamed with fear, the two fainting women lay still.

Then Kadambini, shouting, 'I am not dead, I am not dead,' went down the steps to the zenana well and plunged in. From the upper storey Saradasankar heard the splash.

All night the rain poured; it poured next day at dawn, was pouring still at noon. By dying, Kadambini had proved that she was not dead.

THE SKELETON

In the room next to the one in which we boys used to sleep, there hung a human skeleton. In the night it would rattle in the breeze which played about its bones. In the day these bones were rattled by us. We were taking lessons in osteology from a student in the Campbell Medical School, for our guardians were determined to make us masters of all the sciences. How far they succeeded we need not tell those who know us, and it is better hidden from those who do not.

Many years have passed since then. In the meantime the skeleton has vanished from the room, and the science of osteology from our brains, leaving no trace behind.

The other day, our house was crowded with guests, and I had to pass the night in the same old room. In these now unfamiliar surroundings, sleep refused to come, and, as I tossed from side to side, I heard all the hours of the night chime, one after another, by the church clock nearby. At length the lamp in the corner of the room, after some minutes of choking and spluttering, went out altogether. One or two bereavements had recently happened in the family, so the going out of the lamp naturally led me to thoughts of death. In the great arena of nature, I thought, the light of a lamp losing itself in eternal darkness, and the going out of the light of our little human lives, by day or by night, were much the same thing.

My train of thought recalled to my mind the skeleton. While I was trying to imagine what the body which had clothed it could have been like, it suddenly seemed to me that something was walking round and round my bed, groping along the walls of the room. I could hear its rapid breathing. It seemed as if it was searching for something which it could not find, and pacing round the room with ever-hastier steps. I felt quite sure that this was a mere fancy of my sleepless, excited brain, and that the throbbing of the veins in my temples was really the sound which seemed like running footsteps. Nevertheless, a cold shiver ran all over me. To help get rid of this hallucination, I called out aloud, 'Who is there?'

The footsteps seemed to stop at my bedside, and the reply came, 'It is I. I have come to look for that skeleton of mine.'

It seemed absurd to show any fear before the creature of my own imagination; so, clutching my pillow a little more tightly, I said in a casual sort of way, 'A nice business for this time of night! Of what use will that skeleton be to you now?'

The reply seemed to come almost from my mosquito-curtain itself. 'What a question! In that skeleton were the bones that encircled my heart; the youthful charm of my six-and-twenty years bloomed about it. Should I not desire to see it once more?'

'Of course,' said I, 'a perfectly reasonable desire. Well, go on with your search, while I try to get some sleep.'

Said the voice, 'But I fancy you are lonely. Alright; I'll sit down a while, and we will have a little chat. Years ago I used to sit by men and talk to them. But during the last thirty five years I have only moaned in the wind in the burning places of the dead. I would talk once more with a man as in the old times.'

I felt that someone sat down just near my curtain. Resigning myself to the situation, I replied with as much cordiality as I could summon, 'That will be very nice indeed. Let us talk of something cheerful.'

'The funniest thing I can think of is my own life story. Let me tell you that.'

The church clock chimed the hour of two.

'When I was in the land of the living, and young, I feared one thing like death itself, and that was my husband. My feelings can be likened only to those of a fish caught with a hook. For it was as if a stranger had snatched me away with the sharpest of hooks from the peaceful calm of my childhood's home—and from him I had no means of escape. My husband died two months after my marriage, and my friends and relations moaned pathetically on my behalf. My husband's father, after scrutinising my face with great care, said to my mother-in-law, "Do you not see, she has the evil eye?"—Well, are you listening? I hope you are enjoying the story?'

'Very much indeed!' said I. 'The beginning is extremely humorous.'

'Let me proceed then. I came back to my father's house in great glee. People tried to conceal it from me, but I knew well that I was endowed with a rare and radiant beauty. What is your opinion?'

'Very likely,' I murmured. 'But you must remember that I never saw you.'

'What! Not seen me? What about that skeleton of mine? Ha! ha! ha! Never mind. I was only joking. How can I ever make you believe that those two cavernous hollows contained the brightest of dark, languishing eyes? And that the smile which was revealed by those ruby lips had no resemblance whatsoever to the grinning teeth which you see? The mere attempt to convey to you some idea of the grace, the charm, the soft, firm, dimpled curves, which in the fulness of youth were growing and blossoming over those dry old bones makes me smile; it also makes me angry. The most eminent doctors of my time could not have dreamt of the bones of that body of mine as materials for teaching osteology. Do you know, one young doctor that I knew of actually compared me to a golden champak blossom. It meant that to him the rest of humankind was fit only to illustrate the science of physiology, that I was a flower of beauty. Does anyone think of the skeleton of a champak flower?

'When I walked, I felt that, like a diamond scattering splendour, my every movement set waves of beauty radiating on every side. I used to spend hours gazing on my hands—hands which could gracefully have reined the liveliest of male creatures.

'But that stark and staring old skeleton of mine has borne false witness to you against me, while I was unable to refute the shameless libel. That is why of all men I hate you most! I feel I would like once and for all to banish sleep from your eyes with a vision of that warm rosy loveliness of mine, to sweep out with it all the wretched osteological stuff of which your brain is full.'

'I could have sworn by your body,' cried I, 'if you had it still, that no vestige of osteology has remained in my head, and that the only thing that it is now full of is a radiant vision of perfect loveliness, glowing against the black background of night. I cannot say more than that.'

'I had no girl-companions,' went on the voice. 'My only brother had made up his mind not to marry. In the zenana I was alone. Alone I used to sit in the garden under the shade of the trees, and dream that the whole world was in love with me; that the stars with sleepless gaze were drinking in my beauty, that the wind was languishing in sighs as on some pretext or the other it brushed past me; and that the lawn on which my feet rested, had it been conscious, would have lost consciousness again at their touch. It seemed to me that all the young men in the world were as blades of grass at my feet; and my heart, I know not why, used to grow sad.

'When my brother's friend, Shekhar, had passed out of Medical College, he became our family doctor. I had already often seen him from behind a curtain. My brother was a strange man, and did not care to look on the world with open eyes. It was not empty enough for his taste, so he gradually moved away from it until he was quite lost in an obscure corner. Shekhar was his one friend, so he was the only young man I could ever get to see. And when I held my evening court in my garden, then the host of imaginary young men whom I had at my feet were each one a Shekhar. Are you listening? What are you thinking of?'

I sighed as I replied, 'I was wishing I was Shekhar!'

'Wait a bit. Hear the whole story first. One day, in the rains, I was feverish. The doctor came to see me. That was our first meeting. I was reclining opposite the window, so that the blush of the evening sky might temper the pallor of my complexion. When the doctor, coming in, looked up into my face, I put myself into his place, and gazed at myself in my imagination. I saw in the glorious evening light that delicate wan face laid like a drooping flower against the soft white pillow, with the unrestrained curls playing over the forehead, and the bashfully lowered eyelids casting a pathetic shade over the whole countenance.

'The doctor, in a tone bashfully low, asked my brother, "Might I feel her pulse?"

'I put out a tired, well-rounded wrist from beneath the coverlet. "Ah!" thought I, as I looked on it, "if only there had been a sapphire bracelet." I have never before seen a doctor so awkward about feeling a patient's pulse. His fingers trembled as they felt my wrist. He measured the heat of my fever, I gauged the pulse of his heart. Don't you believe me?'

'Very easily,' said I; 'the human heartbeat tells its tale.'

'After I had been taken ill and restored to health several times, I found that the number of the courtiers who attended my imaginary evening reception began to dwindle till they were reduced to only one! And at last in my little world there remained only one doctor and one patient.

'In these evenings I used to dress myself secretly in a canary-coloured sari; twine about the braided knot into which I did my hair a garland of white jasmine blossoms; and with a little mirror in my hand betake myself to my usual seat under the trees.

'Well! Are you perhaps thinking that the sight of one's own beauty would soon grow wearisome? Ah no! For I did not see myself with my own eyes. I was then one and also two. I used to see myself as though I were the doctor; I gazed, I was charmed, I fell madly in love. But, in spite of all the caresses I lavished on myself, a sigh would wander about my heart, moaning like the evening breeze.

'Anyhow, from that time I was never alone. When I walked I watched with downcast eyes the play of my dainty little toes on the earth, and wondered what the doctor would have felt had he been there to see it. At midday the sky would be filled with the glare of the sun, without a sound, save now and then the distant cry of a passing kite. Outside our garden walls the hawker would pass with his musical cry of "Bangles for sale, crystal bangles". And I, spreading a snow white sheet on the lawn, would lie on it with my head on my arm. With studied carelessness the other arm would rest lightly on the soft sheet, and I would imagine to myself that someone had caught sight of the wonderful pose of my hand, that someone had clasped it in both of his and imprinted a kiss on its rosy palm, and was slowly walking away. What if I ended the story here? How would it do?'

'Not half a bad ending,' I replied thoughtfully. 'It would no doubt remain a little incomplete, but I could easily spend the rest of the night putting in the finishing touches.'

'But that would make the story too serious. Where would the laugh come in? Where would be the skeleton with its grinning teeth?

'So let me go on. As soon as the doctor had got a little practice, he took a room on the ground floor of our house for a consulting chamber. I used to then sometimes ask him jokingly about medicines and poisons, and how much of this drug or that would kill a man. The subject was congenial and he would wax eloquent. These talks familiarised me with the idea of death; and so, love and death were the only two things that filled my little world. My story is now nearly ended—there is not much left.'

'Not much of the night is left either,' I muttered.

'After a time I noticed that the doctor had grown strangely absent-minded, and it seemed as if he were ashamed of something which he was trying to keep from me. One day he came in, somewhat smartly dressed, and borrowed my brother's carriage for the evening.

'My curiosity became too much for me, and I went up to my brother for information. After some talk beside the point, I at last asked him, "By the way, Dada, where is the doctor going this evening in your carriage?"

'My brother briefly replied, "To his death."

'"Oh, do tell me," I importuned. "Where is he really going?"

'"To be married," he said, a little more explicitly.

'"Oh, indeed!" said I, as I laughed long and loud.

'I gradually learnt that the bride was an heiress who would bring the doctor a large sum of money. But why did he insult me by hiding all this from me? Had I ever begged and prayed him not to marry because it would break my heart? Men are not to be trusted. I have known only one man in all my life, and in a moment I made this discovery.

'When the doctor came in after his work and was ready to start, I said to him, rippling with laughter all the while, "Well, doctor, so you are to be married tonight?"

'My gaiety not only made the doctor lose countenance; it thoroughly irritated him.

'"How is it," I went on, "that there is no illumination, no band of music?"

'With a sigh he replied, "Is marriage then such a joyful occasion?"

'I burst out into renewed laughter. "No, no," said I, "this will never do. Who ever heard of a wedding without lights and music?"

'I bothered my brother about it so much that he at once ordered all the trappings of a gay wedding.

'All the time I kept on gaily talking of the bride, of what would happen, of what I would do when the bride came home. "And, doctor," I asked, "will you still go on feeling pulses?" Ha! ha! ha! Though the inner workings of people's, especially men's, minds are not visible, still I can take my oath that these words were piercing the doctor's bosom like deadly darts.

'The marriage was to be celebrated late at night. Before starting, the doctor and my brother were having a glass of wine together on the terrace, as was their daily habit. The moon had just risen.

'I went up smiling, and said, "Have you forgotten your wedding, doctor? It is time to start."

'I must here tell you one little thing. I had meanwhile gone down to the dispensary and got a little powder, which at a convenient opportunity I had dropped unobserved into the doctor's glass.

'The doctor, draining his glass at a gulp, in a voice thick with emotion, and with a look that pierced me to the heart, said, "Then I must go."

'The music struck up. I went into my room and dressed myself in my bridal robes of silk and gold. I took out my jewellery and ornaments from the safe and put them all on; I put the red mark of wifehood on the parting in my hair. And then under the tree in the garden I prepared my bed.

'It was a beautiful night. The gentle south wind was kissing away the weariness of the world. The scent of jasmine and bela filled the garden with rejoicing.

'When the sound of the music began to grow fainter and fainter, the light of the moon got dimmer and dimmer, the world with its lifelong associations of home and kin faded away from my perceptions like some illusion, I closed my eyes, and smiled.

'I fancied that when people came and found me they would see that smile of mine lingering on my lips like a trace of rose-coloured wine, that when I thus slowly entered my eternal bridal chamber I should carry with me this smile, illuminating my face. But alas for the bridal chamber! Alas for the bridal robes of silk and gold! When I woke at the sound of a rattling within me, I found three urchins learning osteology from my skeleton. Where in my bosom my joys and griefs used to throb, and the petals of youth were to open one by one, there the master with his pointer was busy naming my bones. And as to that last smile, which I had so carefully rehearsed, did you see any sign of that? ... Well, how did you like the story?'

'It has been delightful,' said I.

At this point the first crow began to caw. 'Are you there?' I asked. There was no reply.

The morning light entered the room.

THE TRUST PROPERTY

I

Brindaban Kundu came to his father in a rage and said, 'I am off this moment.'

'Ungrateful wretch!' sneered the father, Jaganath Kundu. 'When you have paid me back all that I have spent on your food and clothing, it will be time enough to give yourself these airs.'

Such food and clothing as was customary in Jaganath's household could not have cost very much. Our rishis of old managed to feed and clothe themselves on an incredibly small outlay. Jaganath's behaviour showed that his ideal in these respects was equally high. That he could not fully live up to it was due partly to the bad influence of the degenerate society around him, and partly to certain unreasonable demands of Nature in her attempt to keep body and soul together.

So long as Brindaban was single, things went smoothly enough, but after his marriage he began to depart from the high and rarefied standard cherished by his sire. It was clear that the son's ideas of comfort were moving away from the spiritual to the material, and imitating the ways of the world. He was unwilling to put up with the discomforts of heat and cold, thirst and hunger. His minimum of food and clothing rose apace.

Frequent were the quarrels between the father and the son. At last Brindaban's wife became seriously ill and a kabiraj was called in. But when the doctor prescribed a costly medicine for his patient, Jaganath took it as a proof of sheer incompetence and turned him out immediately. At first Brindaban besought his father to allow the treatment to continue, then he quarrelled with him about it, but to no purpose. When his wife died, he abused his father and called him a murderer.

'Nonsense!' said the father. 'Don't people die even after swallowing all kinds of drugs? If costly medicines could save life, how is it that kings and emperors are not immortal? You don't expect your wife to die with more pomp and ceremony than did your mother and your grandmother before her, do you?'

Brindaban might really have derived a great consolation from these words, had he not been overwhelmed with grief and become incapable of proper thinking. Neither his mother nor his grandmother had taken any medicine before making their exit from this world, and this was the time-honoured custom of the family. But, alas, the younger generation was unwilling to die according to ancient custom. The English had newly come to the country at the time we speak of. Even in those remote days, the good old folks were horrified at the unorthodox ways of the new generation and sat speechless, trying to draw comfort from their hookahs.

Be that as it may, the modern Brindaban said to his old father, 'I am off.'

The father instantly agreed, and wished publicly that, should he ever give his son one single pice in future, the gods might reckon his act as shedding the holy blood of cows. Brindaban in his turn similarly wished that should he ever accept anything from his father, his act might be held as bad as matricide.

The people of the village looked upon this small revolution as a great relief after a long period of monotony. And when Jaganath disinherited his only son, everyone did his best to console him. All were unanimous in the opinion that to quarrel with a father for the sake of a wife was possible only in these degenerate days. And the reason they gave was sound too. 'When your wife dies,' they said, 'you can find a second one without delay. But when your father dies, you can't get another to replace him for love or money.' Their logic no doubt was perfect, but we suspect that the utter hopelessness of getting another father did not trouble the misguided son very much. On the contrary, he looked upon it as a mercy.

Nor did separation from Brindaban weigh heavily on the mind of his father. In the first place, his absence from home reduced the household expenses. Then again, the father was freed from a great anxiety. The fear of being poisoned by his son and heir had always haunted him. When he ate his scanty fare, he could never banish the thought of poison from his mind. This fear had abated somewhat after the death of his daughter-in-law, and now that the son was gone, it disappeared altogether.

But there was one tender spot in the old man's heart. Brindaban had taken away with him his four-year-old son, Gokul Chandra. Now, the expense of keeping the child was comparatively small, and so Jaganath's affection for him was without a drawback. Still, when Brindaban took him away, his grief, sincere as it was, was mingled at first with calculation as to how much he would save a month by the absence of the two, how much the sum would come to in the year, and what would be the capital to bring it in as interest.

But the empty house, without Gokul Chandra in it to make mischief, became more and more difficult for the old man to live in. There was no one now to play tricks upon him when he was engaged in his puja, no one to snatch away his food and eat it, no one to run away with his inkpot when he was writing up his accounts. His daily routine of life, now uninterrupted, became an intolerable burden to him. He thought that this unworried peace was endurable only in the world to come. When he caught sight of the holes made in his quilt by his grandchild, and the pen-and-ink sketches executed by the same artist on his walls, his heart was heavy with grief. Once upon a time he had reproached the boy bitterly because he had torn his dhoti into pieces within the short space of two years; now tears stood in Jaganath's eyes as he gazed upon the dirty remnants lying in the bedroom. He carefully put them away in his safe, and registered a vow that, should Gokul ever come back again, he should not be reprimanded even if he destroyed one dhoti a year.

But Gokul did not return, and poor Jaganath aged rapidly. His empty home seemed emptier every day.

No longer could the old man stay peacefully at home. Even in the middle of the day, when all respectable folks in the village enjoyed their after-dinner siesta, Jaganath could be seen roaming over the village, hookah in hand. The boys, at the sight of him, would give up their play, and, retiring in a body to a safe distance, chant verses composed by a local poet, praising the old gentleman's economical habits. No one ventured to say his real name, lest he should have to go without his meal that day—and so people gave him names after their own fancy. Elderly people called him Jaganash, but the reason why the younger generation preferred to call him a vampire was hard to guess. It may be that the bloodless, dried-up skin of the old man had some physical resemblance to the vampire's.

II

One afternoon, when Jaganath was rambling as usual through the village lanes shaded by mango topes, he saw a boy, apparently a stranger, assuming the captaincy of the village boys and explaining to them the scheme of some new prank. Won by the force of his character and the startling novelty of his ideas, the boys had all sworn allegiance to him. Unlike the others, he did not run away from the old man as he approached, but came quite close to him and began to shake his own chadar. The result was that a live lizard sprang out of it onto the old man's body, ran down his back and off towards the jungle. Sudden fright made the poor man shiver from head to foot, to the great amusement of the other boys, who shouted with glee. Before Jaganath had gone far, cursing and swearing, the gamcha on his shoulder suddenly disappeared, and the next moment it was seen on the head of the new boy, transformed into a turban.

The novel attentions of this manikin came as a great relief to Jaganath. It was long since any boy had taken such freedom with him. After a good deal of coaxing and many fair promises, he at last persuaded the boy to come to him, and this was the conversation which followed,

'What's your name, my boy?'

'Nitai Pal.'

'Where's your home?'

'Won't tell.'

'Who's your father?'

'Won't tell.'

'Why won't you?'

'Because I have run away from home.'

'What made you do it?'

'My father wanted to send me to school.'

It occurred to Jaganath that it would be useless extravagance to send such a boy to school, and his father must have been an impractical fool not to have thought so.

'Well, well,' said Jaganath, 'how would you like to come and stay with me?'

'Don't mind,' said the boy, and forthwith he installed himself in Jaganath's house. He felt as little hesitation as though it were the shadow of a tree by the wayside. And not only that. He began to proclaim his wishes as regards his food and clothing with such coolness that you would have thought he had paid his reckoning in full beforehand; and, when anything went wrong, he did not scruple to quarrel with the old man. It had been easy enough for Jaganath to get the better of his own child; but, now, where another man's child was concerned, he had to acknowledge defeat.

III

The people of the village marvelled when Nitai Pal was unexpectedly made so much of by Jaganath. They felt sure that the old man's end was near, and the prospect of his bequeathing all his property to this unknown brat made their hearts sore. Furious with envy, they determined to do the boy an injury, but the old man took care of him as though he was a rib in his breast.

At times the boy threatened that he would go away, and the old man used to say to him temptingly, 'I will leave you all the property I possess.' Young as he was, the boy fully understood the grandeur of this promise.

The village people then began to make inquiries after the father of the boy. Their hearts melted with compassion for the agonised parents, and they declared that the son must be a rascal to cause them so much suffering. They heaped abuses on his head, but the heat with which they did it betrayed envy rather than a sense of justice.

One day the old man learned from a wayfarer that one Damodar Pal was seeking his lost son, and was even now coming towards the village. Nitai, when he heard this, became very restless and was ready to run away, leaving his future wealth to take care of itself. Jaganath reassured him, saying, 'I mean to hide you where nobody can find you—not even the village people themselves.'

This whetted the curiosity of the boy and he said, 'Oh, where? Do show me.'

'People will know, if I show you now. Wait till it is night,' said Jaganath.

The hope of discovering the mysterious hiding place delighted Nitai. He planned to himself how, as soon as his father had gone away without him, he would have a bet with his comrades, and play hide and seek. Nobody would be able to find him. Wouldn't it be fun? His father, too, would ransack the whole village, and not find him—that would be rare fun also.

At noon, Jaganath shut the boy up in his house and disappeared for some time. When he came home again, Nitai worried him with questions.

No sooner was it dark than Nitai said, 'Grandfather, shall we go now?'

'It isn't night yet,' replied Jaganath.

A little while later the boy exclaimed, 'It is night now, grandfather; come, let's go.'

'The village people haven't gone to bed yet,' whispered Jaganath.

Nitai waited but a moment, and said, 'They have gone to bed now, grandfather; I am sure they have. Let's start now.'

The night advanced. Sleep began to weigh heavily on the eyelids of the poor boy, and it was a hard struggle for him to keep awake. At midnight, Jaganath caught hold of the boy's arm and left the house, groping through the dark lanes of the sleeping village. Not a sound disturbed the stillness, except the occasional howl of a dog, when all the other dogs far and near would join in chorus, or perhaps the flapping of a night bird, scared by the sound of human footsteps at that unusual hour. Nitai trembled with fear, and held Jaganath fast by the arm.

Across many a field they went, and at last came to a jungle where stood a dilapidated temple without a god in it. 'What, here!' exclaimed Nitai in a tone of disappointment. It was nothing like what he had imagined. There was not much mystery about it. Often, since running away from home, he had passed nights in deserted temples like this. It was not a bad place for playing hide and seek; still, it was quite possible that his comrades might track him there.

From the middle of the floor inside, Jaganath removed a slab of stone, and an underground room with a lamp burning in it was revealed to the astonished eyes of the boy. Fear and curiosity assailed his little heart. Jaganath descended by a ladder and Nitai followed him.

Looking around, the boy saw that there were brass ghurras on all sides of him. In the middle lay spread an assan, and in front of it were arranged vermilion, sandalwood paste, flowers and other articles of puja. To satisfy his curiosity, the boy dipped his hand into some of the ghurras and drew out their contents. They was money and gold mohurs.

Jaganath, addressing the boy, said, 'I told you, Nitai, that I would give you all my money. I have not got much—these ghurras are all that I possess. These I will make over to you today.'

The boy jumped with delight. 'All?' he exclaimed. 'You won't take back a rupee, will you?'

'If I do,' said the old man in solemn tones, 'may my hand be attacked with leprosy. But there is one condition. If ever my grandson, Gokul Chandra, or his son, or his grandson, or his great-grandson or any of his progeny should happen to pass this way, then you must make over to him, or to them, every rupee and every mohur here.'

The boy thought that the old man was raving. 'Very well,' he replied.

'Then sit on this assan,' said Jaganath.

'What for?'

'Because puja will be done to you.'

'But why?' said the boy, taken aback.

'This is the rule.'

The boy squatted on the assan as he was told. Jaganath smeared his forehead with sandalwood paste, put a mark of vermilion between his eyebrows, flung a garland of flowers round his neck and began to recite mantras.

To sit there like a god and hear mantras recited made poor Nitai feel very uneasy. 'Grandfather,' he whispered.

But Jaganath did not reply, and went on muttering his incantations.

Finally, with great difficulty he dragged each ghurra before the boy and made him repeat the following vow after him, 'I do solemnly promise that I will make over all this treasure to Gokul Chandra Kundu, the son of Brindaban Kundu, the grandson of Jaganath Kundu, or to the son or to the grandson or to the great-grandson of the said Gokul Chandra Kundu, or to any other progeny of his who may be the rightful heir.'

The boy repeated this over and over again, until he felt stupefied, and his tongue began to grow stiff in his mouth. When the ceremony was over, the air of the cave was laden with the smoke of the earthen lamp and the breath-poison of the two. The boy felt that the roof of his mouth had become dry as dust, and his hands and feet were burning. He was nearly suffocated.

The lamp became dimmer and dimmer, and then went out altogether. In the total darkness that followed, Nitai could hear the old man climbing up the ladder. 'Grandfather, where are you going to?' he asked, greatly distressed.

'I am going now,' replied Jaganath. 'You remain here. No one will be able to find you. Remember the name Gokul Chandra, the son of Brindaban, and the grandson of Jaganath.'

He then withdrew the ladder. In a stifled, agonised voice the boy implored, 'I want to go back to my father.'

Jaganath replaced the slab. He then knelt down and placed his ear on the stone. Nitai's voice was heard once more—"Father"—and then came the sound of some heavy object falling with a bump—and then everything was still.

Having thus placed his wealth in the hands of a yaksha, Jaganath began to cover up the stone with earth. Then he piled broken bricks and loose mortar over it. On top of it he planted turfs of grass and jungle weed. The night was almost spent, but he could not tear himself away from the spot. Now and again he placed his ear to the ground, and tried to listen. It seemed to him that from far far below—from the abysmal depth of the earth's interior—came a wailing. It seemed to him that the night sky was flooded with that one sound, that the sleeping humanity of all the world was awake, and was sitting on its beds, trying to listen.

The old man in his frenzy kept on heaping earth higher and higher. He wanted somehow to stifle that sound, but still he fancied he could hear "Father".

He struck the spot with all his might and said, 'Be quiet—people might hear you.' But still he imagined he heard "Father".

The sun lighted up the eastern horizon. Jaganath then left the temple and came into the open fields.

There, too, somebody called out "Father". Startled at the sound, he turned back and saw his son at his heels.

'Father,' said Brindaban, 'I hear my boy is hiding himself in your house. I must have him back.'

With dilated eyes and a distorted mouth, the old man leaned forward and exclaimed, 'Your boy?'

'Yes, my boy Gokul. He is Nitai Pal now, and I myself go by the name of Damodar Pal. Your fame has spread so widely in the neighbourhood that we were obliged to cover up our origin, lest people should have refused to pronounce our names.'

Slowly the old man lifted both his arms above his head. His fingers began to twitch convulsively, as though he was trying to catch hold of some imaginary object in the air. He then fell on the ground.

When he came to his senses again, he dragged his son towards the ruined temple. When they were both inside it, he said, 'Do you hear any wailing sound?'

'No, I don't,' said Brindaban.

'Just listen very carefully. Do you hear anybody calling out "Father"?'

'No.'

This seemed to relieve him greatly.

From that day forward, he used to go about asking people, 'Do you hear any wailing sound?' They laughed at the raving dotard.

About four years later, Jaganath lay on his death bed. When the light of this world was gradually fading away from his eyes and his breathing became more and more difficult, he suddenly sat up in a state of delirium. Throwing both his hands in the air, he seemed to grope for something, muttering, 'Nitai, who has removed my ladder?'

Unable to find the ladder to climb out of his terrible dungeon, where there was no light and no air to breathe, he fell on his bed once more, and disappeared into that region where no one has ever been found out in the world's eternal game of hide and seek.

SUBHA

When the girl was given the name of Subhashini, who could have guessed that she would prove dumb? Her two elder sisters were Sukeshini and Suhasini, and for the sake of uniformity her father named his youngest girl Subhashini. She was called Subha for short.

Her two elder sisters had been married with the usual cost and difficulty, and now the youngest daughter lay like a silent weight upon the heart of her parents. All the world seemed to think that because she did not speak, she did not feel; it discussed her future and its own anxiety freely in her presence. She had understood from her earliest childhood that God had sent her like a curse to her father's house, so she withdrew herself from ordinary people, and tried to live apart. If only they would all forget her she felt she could endure it. But who can forget pain? Night and day her parents' minds were aching on her account. Especially her mother looked upon her as a deformity in herself. To a mother a daughter is a more closely intimate part of herself than a son can be; and a fault in her is a source of personal shame. Banikantha, Subha's father, loved her rather better than his other daughters; her mother regarded her with aversion as a stain upon her own body.

If Subha lacked speech, she did not lack a pair of large dark eyes, shaded with long lashes; and her lips trembled like a leaf in response to any thought that rose in her mind.

When we express our thoughts in words, the medium is not found easily. There must be a process of translation, which is often inexact, and then we fall into error. But black eyes need no translating; the mind itself throws a shadow upon them. In them thought opens or shuts, shines forth, or goes out in darkness, hangs steadfast like the setting moon, or, like the swift and restless lightning, illumines all quarters of the sky. They who from birth have had no speech other than the trembling of their lips learn a language of the eyes, endless in expression, deep as the sea, clear as the heavens, wherein play dawn and sunset, light and shadow. The dumb have a lonely grandeur like Nature's own. Wherefore the other children almost dreaded Subha, and never played with her. She was silent and companionless as noontide.

The hamlet where she lived was Chandipur. Its river, small for a river of Bengal, kept to its narrow bounds like a daughter of the middle class. This busy streak of water never overflowed its banks, but went about its duties as though it were a member of every family in the villages beside it. On either side were houses and banks shaded with trees. So, stepping from her queenly throne, the river-goddess became a garden deity of each home; and forgetful of herself, performed her task of endless benediction with swift and cheerful foot.

Banikantha's house looked upon the stream. Every hut and stack in the place could be seen by the passing boatmen. I know not if amid these signs of worldly wealth anyone noticed the little girl who, when her work was done, stole away to the waterside and sat there. But here Nature fulfilled her want of speech, and spoke for her. The murmur of the brook, the voice of the village folk, the songs of the boatmen, the crying of the birds and rustle of trees mingled, and were one with the trembling of her heart. They became one vast wave of sound which beat upon her restless soul. This murmur and movement of Nature were the dumb girl's language; that speech of the dark eyes, which the long lashes shaded, was the language of the world about her. From the trees, where the cicalas chirped, to the quiet stars, there was nothing but signs and gestures, weeping and sighing. And in the deep mid-noon, when the boatmen and fisherfolk had gone to their dinner, when the villagers slept, and birds were still, when the ferry-boats were idle, when the great busy world paused in its toil, and became suddenly a lonely, awful giant, then beneath the vast impressive heavens there were only dumb Nature and a dumb girl, sitting very silent—one under the spreading sunlight, the other where a small tree cast its shadow.

But Subha was not altogether without friends. In the stall were two cows, Sarbbashi and Panguli. They had never heard their names from her lips, but they knew her footfall. Though she had no words, she murmured lovingly and they understood her gentle murmuring better than all speech. When she fondled them or scolded or coaxed them, they understood her better than men could do. Subha would come to the shed, and throw her arms round Sarbbashi's neck; she would rub her cheek against her friend's, and Panguli would turn her great kind eyes and lick her face. The girl paid them three regular visits every day, and others that were irregular. Whenever she heard any words that hurt her, she would come to these dumb friends out of due time. It was as though they guessed her anguish of spirit from her quiet look of sadness. Coming close to her, they would rub their horns softly against her arms, and in dumb, puzzled fashion try to comfort her. Besides these two, there were goats and a kitten; but Subha had not the same equality of friendship with them, though they showed the same attachment. Every time it got a chance, night or day, the kitten would jump into her lap and settle down to slumber, and show its appreciation of an aid to sleep as Subha drew her soft fingers over its neck and back.

Subha had a comrade also among the higher animals, and it is hard to say what the girl's relations with him were, for he could speak, and his gift of speech left them without any common language. He was the youngest boy of the Gosains, Pratap by name, an idle fellow. After long efforts, his parents had abandoned the hope that he would ever make his living. Now losers have this advantage, that, though their own folk disapprove of them, they are generally popular with everyone else. Having no work to chain them, they become public property. Just as every town needs an open space where all may breathe, so a village needs two or three gentlemen of leisure, who can give time to all; so that, if we are lazy and want a companion, one is to hand.

Pratap's chief ambition was to catch fish. He managed to waste a lot of time this way, and might be seen almost any afternoon so employed. It was thus most often that he met Subha. Whatever he was about, he liked a companion; and, when one is catching fish, a silent companion is best of all. Pratap respected Subha for her taciturnity, and, as everyone called her Subha, he showed his affection by calling her Su. Subha used to sit beneath a tamarind, and Pratap, a little distance off, would cast his line. Pratap took with him a small allowance of betel, and Subha prepared it for him. And I think that sitting and gazing a long while, she desired ardently to bring some great help to Pratap, to be of real aid, to prove by any means that she was not a useless burden to the world. But there was nothing to do. Then she turned to the Creator in prayer for some rare power, that by an astonishing miracle she might startle Pratap into exclaiming, 'My! I never dreamt our Su could have done this!'

Only think! If Subha had been a water nymph, she might have risen slowly from the river, bringing the gem of a snake's crown to the landing-place. Then, Pratap, leaving his paltry fishing, might dive into the lower world, and see there, on a golden bed in a palace of silver, whom else but dumb little Su, Banikantha's child? Yes, our Su, the only daughter of the king of that shining city of jewels! But that might not be; it was impossible. Not that anything is really impossible, but Su had been born not into the royal house of Patalpur, but into Banikantha's family, and she knew no means of astonishing the Gosains' boy.

Gradually she grew up. Gradually she began to find herself. A new inexpressible consciousness like a tide from the central places of the sea, when the moon is full, swept through her. She saw herself, questioned herself, but no answer came that she could understand.

Once upon a time, late on a night of full moon, she slowly opened her door and peeped out timidly. Nature, herself at full moon, like lonely Subha, was looking down on the sleeping earth. Her strong young life beat within her; joy and sadness filled her being to its brim; she reached the limits even of her own illimitable loneliness, nay, passed beyond them. Her heart was heavy, and she could not speak! At the skirts of this silent, troubled Mother there stood a silent troubled girl.

The thought of her marriage filled her parents with anxious care. People blamed them, and even talked of making them outcasts. Banikantha was well off; they had fish curry twice daily, and consequently he did not lack enemies. Then the women interfered, and Bani went away for a few days. Presently he returned and said, 'We must go to Calcutta.'

They got ready to go to this strange country. Subha's heart was heavy with tears, like a mist-wrapped dawn. With a vague fear that had been gathering for days, she dogged her father and mother like a dumb animal. With her large eyes wide open, she scanned their faces as though she wished to learn something. But not a word did they vouchsafe. One afternoon in the midst of all this, as Pratap was fishing, he laughed, 'So then, Su, they have caught your bridegroom, and you are going to be married! Mind you don't forget me altogether!' Then he turned his mind again to his fish. As a stricken doe looks in the hunter's face, asking in silent agony, 'What have I done to you?' Subha looked at Pratap. That day she sat no longer beneath her tree. Banikantha, having finished his nap, was smoking in his bedroom when Subha dropped down at his feet and burst out weeping as she gazed towards him. Banikantha tried to comfort her, and his cheek grew wet with tears.

It was settled that on the morrow they should go to Calcutta. Subha went to the cowshed to bid farewell to her childhood's comrades. She fed them with her hand; she clasped their necks, she looked into their faces, and tears fell fast from the eyes which spoke for her. That night was the tenth of the moon. Subha left her room and flung herself down on her grassy couch beside her dear river. It was as if she threw her arms about Earth, her strong, silent mother, and tried to say, 'Do not let me leave you, mother. Put your arms about me, as I have put mine about you, and hold me fast.'

One day in a house in Calcutta, Subha's mother dressed her up with great care. She imprisoned her hair, knotting it up in laces, she hung her about with ornaments, and did her best to kill her natural beauty. Subha's eyes filled with tears. Her mother, fearing they would grow swollen with weeping, scolded her harshly, but the tears disregarded the scolding. The bridegroom came with a friend to inspect the bride. Her parents were dizzy with anxiety and fear when they saw the god arrive to select the beast for his sacrifice. Behind the stage, the mother called her instructions aloud, and her daughter's weeping increased twofold before she sent her into the examiner's presence. The great man, after scanning her a long time, observed, 'Not so bad.'

He took special note of her tears, and thought she must have a tender heart. He put it to her credit in the account, arguing that the heart, which today was distressed at leaving her parents, would presently prove a useful possession. Like the oyster's pearls, the child's tears only increased her value, and he made no other comment.

The almanac was consulted, and the marriage took place on an auspicious day. Having delivered over their dumb girl into another's hands, Subha's parents returned home. Thank God! Their caste in this and their safety in the next world were assured! The bridegroom's work lay in the west, and shortly after the marriage he took his wife thither.

In less than ten days every one knew that the bride was dumb! At least, if any one did not, it was not her fault, for she deceived no one. Her eyes told them everything, though no one understood her. She looked on every hand; she found no speech; she missed the faces, familiar from birth, of those who had understood a dumb girl's language. In her silent heart there sounded an endless, voiceless weeping, which only the Searcher of Hearts could hear.

Using both eyes and ears this time, her lord made another careful examination, and married a second wife who could speak.

THE RIVER STAIRS

If you wish to hear of days gone by, sit on this step of mine, and lend your ears to the murmur of the rippling water.

The month of Ashwin (September) was about to begin. The river was in full flood. Only four of my steps peeped above the surface. The water had crept up to the low-lying parts of the bank, where the kachu plant grew dense beneath the branches of the mango grove. At that bend of the river, three old brick-heaps towered above the water around them. The fishing boats, moored to the trunks of the babla trees on the bank, rocked on the heaving flow-tide at dawn. The path of tall grasses on the sandbank had caught the newly risen sun; they had just begun to flower, and were not yet in full bloom.

The little boats puffed out their tiny sails on the sunlit river. The Brahmin priest had come to bathe with his ritual vessels. The women arrived in twos and threes to draw water. I knew this was the time of Kusum's coming to the bathing stairs.

But that morning I missed her. Bhuban and Swarno mourned at the ghat. They said that their friend had been led away to her husband's house, which was a place far away from the river, with strange people, strange houses and strange roads.

In time she almost faded out of my mind. A year passed. The women at the ghat now rarely talked of Kusum. But one evening I was startled by the touch of the long familiar feet. Ah, yes, but those feet were now without anklets, they had lost their old music.

Kusum had become a widow. They said that her husband had worked in some far-off place, and that she had met him only once or twice. A letter brought her the news of his death. A widow at eight years old, she had rubbed out the wife's red mark from her forehead, stripped off her bangles and come back to her old home by the Ganges. But she found few of her old playmates there. Of them, Bhuban, Swarno and Amala were married and gone away; only Sarat remained, and she too, they said, would be wed in December next.

As the Ganges rapidly grows to fulness with the coming of the rains, so did Kusum day by day grow to the fulness of beauty and youth. But her dull-coloured robe, pensive face and quiet manners drew a veil over her youth, and hid it from men's eyes as in a mist. Ten years slipped by, and none seemed to have noticed that Kusum had grown up.

One morning such as this, at the end of a far-off September, a tall, young, fair-skinned Sanyasi, coming I know not whence, took shelter in the Shiva temple in front of me. His arrival was talked about in the village. The women left their pitchers behind, and crowded into the temple to bow to the holy man.

The crowd increased day by day. The Sanyasi's fame rapidly spread among womenkind. One day he would recite the Gita, another day talk about a holy book in the temple. Some sought him for counsel, some for spells, some for medicines.

Many months passed away. In April, at the time of the solar eclipse, vast crowds came here to bathe in the Ganges. A fair was held under the babla tree. Many of the pilgrims went to visit the Sanyasi, and among them were a party of women from the village where Kusum had been married.

It was morning. The Sanyasi was counting his beads on my steps, when, all of a sudden, one of the women pilgrims nudged another, and said, 'Why! He is our Kusum's husband!' Another parted her veil a little in the middle with two fingers and cried out, 'Oh dear me! So it is! He is the younger son of the Chatterji family of our village!' Said a third, who made little parade of her veil, 'Ah! he has got exactly the same brow, nose and eyes!' Yet another woman, without turning to the Sanyasi, stirred the water with her pitcher and sighed, 'Alas! That young man is no more; he will not come back. Bad luck to Kusum!'

'But,' objected one, 'he had not such a big beard.' Another said, 'He was not so thin,' and yet another, 'He was most probably not so tall.' That settled the question for the time, and the matter spread no further.

One evening, as the full moon rose, Kusum came and sat upon my last step above the water and cast her shadow upon me.

There was no other at the ghat just then. The crickets were chirping about me. The din of brass gongs and bells had ceased in the temple—the last wave of sound grew fainter and fainter, until it merged like the shade of a sound in the dim groves of the farther bank. On the dark water of the Ganges lay a line of glistening moonlight. On the bank above, in bush and hedge, under the porch of the temple, in the base of ruined houses, by the side of the tank, in the palm grove, gathered shadows of fantastic shape. The bats swung from the chhatim boughs. Near the houses the loud clamour of the jackals rose and sank into silence.

Slowly the Sanyasi came out of the temple. Descending a few steps of the ghat he saw a woman sitting alone, and was about to go back when suddenly Kusum raised her head and looked behind her. The veil slipped away from her. The moonlight fell upon her face as she looked up.

The owl flew away hooting over their heads. Starting at the sound, Kusum came to herself and put the veil back on her head. Then she bowed low at the Sanyasi's feet.

He gave her his blessing and asked, 'Who are you?'

She replied, 'I am Kusum.'

No other word was spoken that night. Kusum went slowly back to her house. But the Sanyasi remained sitting on my steps for long hours that night. At last when the moon passed from the east to the west, and the Sanyasi's shadow, shifting from behind, fell in front of him, he rose and entered the temple.

Henceforth I saw Kusum come daily to bow at his feet. When he expounded the holy books, she stood in a corner, listening to him. After finishing his morning service, he used to call her to himself and speak on religion. She could not have understood it all; but, listening attentively in silence, she tried to understand it. As he directed her, so she acted implicitly. She served daily at the temple—ever alert in the god's worship—gathering flowers for the puja, and drawing water from the Ganges to wash the temple floor.

The winter was drawing to a close. We had cold winds. But now and then in the evening the warm spring breeze would blow unexpectedly from the south; the sky would lose its chilly aspect, pipes would sound, and music be heard in the village after a long silence. The boatmen would set their boats drifting down the current, stop rowing, and begin to sing the songs of Krishna. This was the season.

Just then I began to miss Kusum. For sometime she had given up visiting the temple, the ghat, or the Sanyasi.

What happened next I do not know, but after a while the two met together on my steps one evening.

With downcast looks, Kusum asked, 'Master, did you send for me?'

'Yes, why do I not see you? Why have you grown neglectful of late in serving the gods?'

She kept silent.

'Tell me your thoughts without reserve.'

Half averting her face, she replied, 'I am a sinner, Master, and hence I have failed in the worship.'

The Sanyasi said, 'Kusum, I know there is unrest in your heart.'

She gave a slight start, and, drawing the end of her sari over her face, she sat down on the step at the Sanyasi's feet and wept.

He moved a little way, and said, 'Tell me what you have in your heart, and I shall show you the way to peace.'

She replied in a tone of unshaken faith, stopping now and then for words, 'If you bid me, I must speak out. But, then, I cannot explain it clearly. You, Master, must have guessed it all. I adored one as a god, I worshipped him, and the bliss of that devotion filled my heart to fulness. But one night I dreamt that the lord of my heart was sitting in a garden somewhere, clasping my right hand in his left, and whispering to me of love. The whole scene did not appear to me at all strange. The dream vanished, but its hold on me remained. Next day when I beheld him he appeared in another light than before. That dream picture continued to haunt my mind. I fled far from him in fear, and the picture clung to me. Since then my heart has known no peace—all has grown dark within me!'

While she was wiping her tears and telling this tale, I felt that the Sanyasi was firmly pressing my stone surface with his right foot.

Her speech done, the Sanyasi said, 'You must tell me who you saw in your dream.'

With folded hands, she entreated, 'I cannot.'

He insisted, 'You must tell me who he was.'

Wringing her hands, she asked, 'Must I tell it?'

He replied, 'Yes, you must.'

Then crying, 'You are he, Master!' she fell on her face on my stony bosom and sobbed.

When she came to herself and sat up, the Sanyasi said slowly, 'I am leaving this place tonight that you may not see me again. Know that I am a Sanyasi, not belonging to this world. You must forget me.'

Kusum replied in a low voice. 'It will be so, Master.'

The Sanyasi said, 'I take my leave.'

Without a word more, Kusum bowed to him, and placed the dust of his feet on her head. He left the place.

The moon set; the night grew dark. I heard a splash in the water. The wind raved in the darkness, as if it wanted to blow out all the stars of the sky.

MY FAIR NEIGHBOUR

My feelings towards the young widow who lived in the next house to mine were feelings of worship; at least, that is what I told my friends and myself. Even my nearest intimate, Nabin, knew nothing of the real state of my mind. And I had a sort of pride that I could keep my passion pure by thus concealing it in the inmost recesses of my heart. She was like a dew-drenched sephali-blossom, untimely fallen to earth. Too radiant and holy for the flower-decked marriage bed, she had been dedicated to Heaven.

But passion is like the mountain stream, and refuses to be enclosed in the place of its birth; it must seek an outlet. That is why I tried to give expression to my emotions in poems; but my unwilling pen refused to desecrate the object of my worship.

It happened curiously that just at this time my friend Nabin was afflicted with a madness of verse. It came upon him like an earthquake. It was the poor fellow's first attack, and he was equally unprepared for rhyme and rhythm. Nevertheless, he could not refrain, for he succumbed to the fascination, as a widower to his second wife.

So Nabin sought help from me. The subject of his poems was the old, old one, which is ever new: his poems were all addressed to the beloved one. I slapped his back in jest, and asked him, 'Well, old chap, who is she?'

Nabin laughed as he replied, 'That I have not yet discovered!'

I confess that I found considerable comfort in bringing help to my friend. Like a hen brooding on a duck's egg, I lavished all the warmth of my pent-up passion on Nabin's effusions. So vigorously did I revise and improve his crude productions that the larger part of each poem became my own.

Then Nabin would say in surprise, 'That is just what I wanted to say, but could not. How on earth do you manage to get hold of all these fine sentiments?'

Poet-like, I would reply, 'They come from my imagination; for, as you know, truth is silent, and it is imagination only which waxes eloquent. Reality represses the flow of feeling like a rock; imagination cuts out a path for itself.'

And the poor puzzled Nabin would say, 'Y-e-s, I see, yes, of course'; and then after some thought, would murmur again, 'Yes, yes, you are right!'

As I have already said, in my own love there was a feeling of reverential delicacy which prevented me from putting it in words. But with Nabin as a screen, there was nothing to hinder the flow of my pen; and a true warmth of feeling gushed out into these vicarious poems.

Nabin, in his lucid moments, would say, 'But these are yours! Let me publish them over your name.'

'Nonsense!' I would reply. 'They are yours, my dear fellow; I have only added a touch or two here and there.'

And Nabin gradually came to believe it.

I will not deny that, with a feeling akin to that of the astronomer gazing into the starry heavens, I did sometimes turn my eyes towards the window of the house next door. It is also true that now and again my furtive glances would be rewarded with a vision. And the least glimpse of the pure light of that countenance would at once still and clarify all that was turbulent and unworthy in my emotions.

But one day I was startled. Could I believe my eyes? It was a hot summer afternoon. One of the fierce and fitful nor'westers was threatening. Black clouds were massed in the north-west corner of the sky; and against the strange and fearful light of that background my fair neighbour stood, gazing out into empty space. And what a world of forlorn longing did I discover in the far-away look of those lustrous black eyes! Was there then, perchance, still some living volcano within the serene radiance of that moon of mine?

Alas! That look of limitless yearning, which was winging its way through the clouds like an eager bird, surely sought—not heaven—but the nest of some human heart!

At the sight of the unutterable passion of that look I could hardly contain myself. I was no longer satisfied with correcting crude poems. My whole being longed to express itself in some worthy action. At last I thought I would devote myself to making widow-remarriage popular in my country. I was prepared not only to speak and write on the subject, but also to spend money on its cause.

Nabin began to argue with me. 'Permanent widowhood,' said he, 'has in it a sense of immense purity and peace; a calm beauty like that of the silent places of the dead shimmering in the wan light of the eleventh moon. Would not the mere possibility of remarriage destroy its divine beauty?'

Now this sort of sentimentality always makes me furious. In times of famine, if a well-fed man speaks scornfully of food, and advises a starving man at the point of death to glut his hunger on the fragrance of flowers and the song of birds, what are we to think of him?

I said with some heat, 'Look here, Nabin, to the artist a ruin may be a beautiful object; but houses are built not only for the contemplation of artists, but that people may live therein. So they have to be kept in repair in spite of artistic susceptibilities. It is all very well for you to idealise widowhood from your safe distance, but you should remember that within widowhood there is a sensitive human heart, throbbing with pain and desire.'

I had an impression that the conversion of Nabin would be a difficult matter, so perhaps I was more impassioned than I need have been. I was somewhat surprised to find at the conclusion of my little speech that Nabin, after a single thoughtful sigh, completely agreed with me.

After about a week Nabin came to me, and said that if I would help him he was prepared to lead the way by marrying a widow himself.

I was overjoyed. I embraced him effusively, and promised him any money that might be required for the purpose. Then Nabin told me his story.

I learned that Nabin's loved one was not an imaginary being. It appeared that Nabin, too, had for some time adored a widow from a distance, but had not spoken of his feelings to any living soul. Then the magazines in which Nabin's poems, or rather my poems, used to appear had reached the fair one's hands; and the poems had not been ineffective.

Not that Nabin had deliberately intended, as he was careful to explain, to conduct love-making in that way. In fact, said he, he had no idea that the widow knew how to read. He used to post the magazine, without disclosing the sender's name, addressed to the widow's brother. It was only a sort of fancy of his, a concession to his hopeless passion. It was flinging garlands before a deity; it is not the worshipper's affair whether the god knows or not, whether he accepts or ignores the offering.

And Nabin particularly wanted me to understand that he had no definite end in view when on diverse pretexts he sought and made the acquaintance of the widow's brother. Any near relation of the loved one needs must have a special interest for the lover.

Then followed a long story about how an illness of the brother at last brought them together. The presence of the poet himself naturally led to much discussion of the poems; nor was the discussion necessarily restricted to the subject out of which it arose.

After his recent defeat in argument at my hands, Nabin had mustered up the courage to propose marriage to the widow. At first he could not gain her consent. But when he had made full use of my eloquent words, supplemented by a tear or two of his own, the fair one capitulated unconditionally. Some money was now wanted by her guardian to make arrangements.

'Take it at once,' said I.

'But,' Nabin went on, 'you know it will be some months before I can appease my father sufficiently for him to continue my allowance. How are we to live in the meantime?'

I wrote out the necessary cheque without a word, and then I said, 'Now tell me who she is. You need not look on me as a possible rival, for I swear I will not write poems to her; and even if I do I will not send them to her brother, but to you!'

'Don't be absurd,' said Nabin; 'I have not kept back her name because I feared your rivalry! The fact is, she was very much perturbed at taking this unusual step, and had asked me not to talk about the matter to my friends. But it no longer matters, now that everything has been satisfactorily settled. She lives at no 19, the house next to yours.'

If my heart had been an iron boiler it would have burst. 'So she has no objection to remarriage?' I simply asked.

'Not at the present moment,' replied Nabin with a smile.

'And was it the poems alone which wrought the magic change?'

'Well, my poems were not so bad, you know,' said Nabin, 'were they?'

I swore mentally.

But at whom was I to swear? At him? At myself? At Providence? All the same, I swore.

THE KINGDOM OF CARDS

I

Once upon a time there was a lonely island in a distant sea where lived the Kings and Queens, the Aces and the Knaves, in the Kingdom of Cards. The Tens and Nines, with the Twos and Threes, and all the other members, had long ago settled there also. But these were not twice-born people, like the famous Court Cards.

The Ace, the King and the Knave were the three highest castes. The fourth Caste was made up of a mixture of the lower Cards. The Twos and Threes were lowest of all. These inferior Cards were never allowed to sit in the same row with the great Court Cards.

Wonderful indeed were the regulations and rules of that island kingdom. The particular rank of each individual had been settled from time immemorial. Everyone had his own appointed work, and never did anything else. An unseen hand appeared to be directing them wherever they went, according to the Rules.

No one in the Kingdom of Cards had any occasion to think: no one had any need to come to any decision: no one was ever required to debate any new subject. The citizens all moved along in a listless groove without speech. When they fell, they made no noise. They lay down on their backs and gazed upward at the sky with each prim feature firmly fixed forever.

There was a remarkable stillness in the Kingdom of Cards. Satisfaction and contentment were complete in all their rounded wholeness. There was never any uproar or violence. There was never any excitement or enthusiasm.

The great ocean, crooning its lullaby with one unceasing melody, lapped the island to sleep with a thousand soft touches of its wave's white hands. The vast sky, like the outspread azure wings of the brooding mother bird, nestled the island round with its downy plume. For on the distant horizon a deep blue line betokened another shore. But no sound of quarrel or strife could reach the Island of Cards, to break its calm repose.

II

In that far-off foreign land across the sea, there lived a young Prince whose mother was a sorrowing queen. This queen had fallen from favour, and was living with her only son on the seashore. The Prince passed his childhood alone and forlorn, sitting by his forlorn mother, weaving the net of his big desires. He longed to go in search of the Flying Horse, the Jewel in the Cobra's hood, the Rose of Heaven, the Magic Roads, or to find where the Princess Beauty was sleeping in the Ogre's castle over the thirteen rivers and across the seven seas.

From the Son of the Merchant at school the young Prince learnt the stories of foreign kingdoms. From the Son of the Kotwal he learnt the adventures of the Two Genii of the Lamp. And when the rain came beating down, and the clouds covered the sky, he would sit on the threshold facing the sea, and say to his sorrowing mother, 'Tell me, mother, a story of some very far-off land.'

And his mother would tell him an endless tale she had heard in her childhood of a wonderful country beyond the sea where dwelt the Princess Beauty. And the heart of the young Prince would become sick with longing, as he sat on the threshold, looking out on the ocean, listening to his mother's wonderful story, while the rain outside came beating down and the grey clouds covered the sky.

One day the Son of the Merchant came to the Prince, and said boldly, 'Comrade, my studies are over. I am now setting out on my travels to seek my fortunes on the sea. I have come to bid you goodbye.'

The Prince said, ‘I will go with you.’

And the Son of Kotwal said, ‘Comrades, trusty and true, you will not leave me behind. I also will be your companion.’

Then the young Prince said to his sorrowing mother, ‘Mother, I am now setting out on my travels to seek my fortune. When I come back once more, I shall surely have found some way to remove all your sorrows.’

So the Three Companions set out on their travels together. In the harbour were anchored the twelve ships of the merchant, and the Three Companions got on board. The south wind was blowing, and the twelve ships sailed away, as fast as the desires which rose in the Prince’s breast.

At the Conch Shell Island they filled one ship with conches. At the Sandalwood Island they filled a second ship with sandalwood, and at the Coral Island they filled a third ship with coral.

Four years passed, and they filled four more ships, one with ivory, one with musk, one with cloves and one with nutmegs.

But when these ships were all loaded, a terrible tempest arose. The ships were all of them sunk, with their cloves and nutmeg, and musk and ivory, and coral and sandalwood and conches. But the ship with the Three Companions struck on an island reef buried them safe ashore, and itself broke in pieces.

This was the famous Island of Cards, where lived the Ace and King and Queen and Knave, with the Nines and Tens and all the other members—according to the Rules.

III

Up till now there had been nothing to disturb that island stillness. No new thing had ever happened. No discussion had ever been held.

And then, of a sudden, the Three Companions appeared, thrown up by the sea—and the Great Debate began. There were three main points of dispute.

First, to what caste should these unclassed strangers belong? Should they rank with the Court Cards? Or were they merely lower caste people, to be ranked with the Nines and Tens? No precedent could be quoted to decide this weighty question.

Secondly, what was their clan? Had they the fairer hue and bright complexion of the Hearts, or was theirs the darker complexion of the Clubs? Over this question there were interminable disputes. The whole marriage system of the island, with its intricate regulations, would depend on its nice adjustment.

Thirdly, what food should they take? With whom should they live and sleep? And should their heads be placed south-west, north-west, or only north-east? In all the Kingdom of Cards, a series of problems so vital and critical had never been debated before.

But the Three Companions grew desperately hungry. They had to get food in some way or the other. So while this debate went on, with its interminable silence and pauses, and while the Aces called their own meeting, and formed themselves into a Committee, to find some obsolete dealing with the question, the Three Companions themselves were eating all they could find, and drinking out of every vessel, and breaking all regulations.

Even the Twos and Threes were shocked at this outrageous behaviour. The Threes said, 'Brother Twos, these people are openly shameless!' And the Twos said, 'Brother Threes, they are evidently of lower caste than ourselves!' After their meal was over, the Three Companions went for a stroll in the city.

When they saw the ponderous people moving in their dismal processions with prim and solemn faces, the Prince turned to the Son of the Merchant and the Son of the Kotwal, and threw back his head, and gave one stupendous laugh.

Down Royal Street and across Ace Square and along the Knave Embankment ran the quiver of this strange, unheard-of laughter, the laughter that, amazed at itself, expired in the vast vacuum of silence.

The Son of the Kotwal and the Son of the Merchant were chilled through to the bone by the ghost-like stillness around them. They turned to the Prince, and said, 'Comrade, let us away. Let us not stop for a moment in this awful land of ghosts.'

But the Prince said, 'Comrades, these people resemble men, so I am going to find out, by shaking them upside down and outside in, whether they have a single drop of warm living blood left in their veins.'

IV

The days passed one by one, and the placid existence of the Island went on, almost without a ripple. The Three Companions obeyed no rules or regulations. They never did anything correctly either in sitting or standing or turning themselves round or lying on their back. On the contrary, wherever they saw these things going on precisely and exactly according to the Rules, they gave way to inordinate laughter. They remained unimpressed altogether by the eternal gravity of those eternal regulations.

One day the great Court Cards came to the Son of the Kotwal and the Son of the Merchant and the Prince.

'Why,' they asked slowly, 'are you not moving according to the Rules?'

The Three Companions answered, 'Because that is our Ichcha (wish).'

The great Court Cards with hollow, cavernous voices, as if slowly awakening from an age-long dream, said together, 'Ichcha! And pray who is Ichcha?'

They could not understand who Ichcha was then, but the whole island was to understand it by and by. The first glimmer of light passed the threshold of their minds when they found out, through watching the actions of the Prince, that they might move in a straight line in an opposite direction from the one in which they had always gone before. Then they made another startling discovery, that there was another side to the Cards which they had never yet noticed with attention. This was the beginning of the change.

Now that the change had begun, the Three Companions were able to initiate them more and more deeply into the mysteries of Ichcha. The Cards gradually became aware that life was not bound by regulations. They began to feel a secret satisfaction in the kingly power of choosing for themselves.

But with this first impact of Ichcha the whole pack of cards began to totter slowly, and then tumble down to the ground. The scene was like that of some huge python awakening from a long sleep, as it slowly unfolds its numberless coils with a quiver that runs through its whole frame.

V

Hitherto the Queens of Spades and Clubs and Diamonds and Hearts had remained behind curtains with eyes that gazed vacantly into space, or else remained fixed upon the ground.

And now, all of a sudden, on an afternoon in spring the Queen of Hearts from the balcony raised her dark eyebrows for a moment, and cast a single glance upon the Prince from the corner of her eye.

'Great God,' cried the Prince, 'I thought they were all painted images. But I am wrong. They are women, after all.'

Then the young Prince called to his side his two Companions, and said in a meditative voice, 'My comrades! There is a charm about these ladies that I never noticed before. When I saw that glance of the Queen's dark, luminous eyes, brightening with new emotion, it seemed to me like the first faint streak of dawn in a newly created world.'

The two Companions smiled a knowing smile, and said, 'Is that really so, Prince?'

And the poor Queen of Hearts from that day went from bad to worse. She began to forget all rules in a truly scandalous manner. If, for instance, her place in the row was beside the Knave, she suddenly found herself quite accidentally standing beside the Prince instead. At this, the Knave, with motionless face and solemn voice, would say, 'Queen, you have made a mistake.'

And the poor Queen of Hearts' red cheeks would get redder than ever. But the Prince would come gallantly to her rescue and say, 'No! There is no mistake. From today I am going to be Knave!'

Now it came to pass that, while everyone was trying to correct the improprieties of the guilty Queen of Hearts, they began to make mistakes themselves. The Aces found themselves elbowed out by the Kings. The Kings got muddled up with the Knaves. The Nines and Tens assumed airs as though they belonged to the Great Court Cards. The Twos and Threes were found secretly taking the places specially resented for the Fours and Fives. Confusion had never been so confounded before.

Many spring seasons had come and gone in that Island of Cards. The Kokil, the bird of Spring, had sung its song year after year. But it had never stirred the blood as it stirred it now. In days gone by, the sea had sung its tireless melody. But, then, it had proclaimed only the inflexible monotony of the Rule. And suddenly, its waves were telling, through all their flashing light and luminous shade and myriad voices, the deepest yearnings of the heart of love!

VI

Where are vanished now their prim, round, regular, complacent features? Here is a face full of love-sick longing. Here is a heart beating wild with regrets. Here is a mind racked sore with doubts. Music and sighing, and smiles and tears, are filling the air. Life is throbbing; hearts are breaking, passions are kindling.

Everyone is now thinking of his own appearance, and comparing himself with others. The Ace of Clubs is musing to himself that the King of Spades may be just passably good-looking. 'But,' says he, 'when I walk down the street, you have only to see how people's eyes turn towards me.' The King of Spades is saying, 'Why on earth is that Ace of Clubs always straining his neck and strutting about like a peacock? He imagines all the Queens are dying of love for him, while the real fact is—' Here he pauses, and examines his face in the glass.

But the Queens were the worst of all. They began to spend all their time in dressing themselves up to the Nines. And the Nines would become their hopeless and abject slaves. But their cutting remarks about one another were more shocking still.

So the young men would sit listless on the leaves under the trees, lolling with outstretched limbs in the forest shade. And the young maidens, dressed in pale blue robes, would come walking accidentally to the same shade of the same forest by the same trees, and turn their eyes as though they saw no one there, and look as though they came out to see nothing at all. And then one young man more forward than the rest in a fit of madness would dare to go near to a maiden in blue. But, as he drew near, speech would forsake him. He would stand there tongue-tied and foolish, and the favourable moment would pass.

The Kokil birds were singing in the boughs overhead. The mischievous south wind was blowing; it disarrayed the hair, it whispered in the ear, and stirred the music in the blood. The leaves of the trees were murmuring with rustling delight. And the ceaseless sound of the ocean made all the mute longings of the heart of man and maid surge backwards and forwards on the full springtide of love.

The Three Companions had brought into the dried-up channels of the Kingdom of Cards the full flood-tide of a new life.

VII

And, though the tide was full, there was a pause as though the rising waters would not break into foam but remain suspended forever. There were no outspoken words, only a cautious going forward one step and receding two. All seemed busy heaping up their unfulfilled desires like castles in the air, or fortresses of sand. They were pale and speechless, their eyes were burning, their lips trembling with unspoken secrets.

The Prince saw what was wrong. He summoned everyone on the Island and said, 'Bring hither the flutes and the cymbals, the pipes and drums. Let all be played together, and raise loud shouts of rejoicing. For the Queen of Hearts this very night is going to choose her Mate!'

So the Tens and Nines began to blow on their flutes and pipes; the Eights and Sevens played on their sackbuts and viols; and even the Twos and Threes began to beat madly on their drums.

When this tumultous gust of music came, it swept away at one blast all those sighings and mopings. And then what a torrent of laughter and words poured forth! There were daring proposals and locking refusals, and gossip and chatter, and jests and merriment. It was like the swaying and shaking, and rustling and soughing, in a summer gale, of a million leaves and branches in the depth of the primeval forest.

But the Queen of Hearts, in a rose-red robe, sat silent in the shadow of her secret bower, and listened to the great uproarious sound of music and mirth that came floating towards her. She shut her eyes and dreamt her dream of lore. And when she opened them she found the Prince seated on the ground before her, gazing up at her face. And she covered her eyes with both hands and shrank back, quivering with an inward tumult of joy.

And the Prince passed the whole day alone, walking by the side of the surging sea. He carried in his mind that startled look, that shrinking gesture of the Queen, and his heart beat high with hope.

That night the serried, gaily-dressed ranks of young men and maidens waited with smiling faces at the Palace Gates. The Palace Hall was lighted with fairy lamps and festooned with the flowers of spring. Slowly the Queen of

Hearts entered, and the whole assembly rose to greet her. With a jasmine garland in her hand, she stood before the Prince with downcast eyes. In her lowly bashfulness she could hardly raise the garland to the neck of the Mate she had chosen. But the Prince bowed his head, and the garland slipped to its place. The assembly of youths and maidens had waited her choice with eager, expectant hush. And when the choice was made, the whole vast concourse rocked and swayed with a tumult of wild delight. And the sound of their shouts was heard in every part of the island, and by ships far out at sea. Never had such a shout been raised in the Kingdom of Cards before.

And they carried the Prince and his Bride, and seated them on the throne, and crowned them then and there in the Ancient Island of Cards.

And the sorrowing Mother Queen, on the far-off island shore on the other side of the sea, came sailing to her son's new kingdom in a ship adorned with gold.

And the citizens are no longer regulated according to the Rules, but are good or bad, or both, according to their Ichcha.

About the Author

Rabindranath Tagore was a Bengali poet, short story writer, song composer, playwright, essayist and painter who introduced Indian culture to the West and vice versa. In 1913 he became the first non-European to receive the Nobel Prize for Literature. Known mostly for his poetry, Tagore wrote novels, essays, short stories, travelogues, dramas, and thousands of songs. Of Tagore's prose, his short stories are the most highly regarded. He is credited with originating the Bengali-language version of the genre.